Sherlock Holmes
and the Secret Seven

Sherlock Holmes and the Secret Seven

Val Andrews

**BREESE
BOOKS
LONDON**

First published in 2001 by
Breese Books Ltd
164 Kensington Park Road, London W11 2ER, England

ISBN: 0 947533 09 5

Front cover photograph
is reproduced by kind permission of
Retrograph Archive, London

Typeset in 11½/14pt Caslon by
Ann Buchan (Typesetters), Middlesex
Printed in the United States of America

CHAPTER 1

An Introduction to the Secret Seven

'Those steps upon the stairs, Watson, can you tell me anything of the person who makes them?'

My wife having gone to stay with a relative in Australia, I had decided to accept an invitation from my friend Mr Sherlock Holmes to stay with him at the old rooms that we had once shared in Baker Street. I was out of practice with the methods which I knew of old, but here he was asking me to enter into the process of deduction not an hour after I had arrived.

I laughed. 'Upon my word, I have only just unpacked my carpet bag and you put me to the test. Well, I believe, unlikely as it sounds, that you have a visit from a Chinese mandarin!'

He nodded shrewdly. 'You base your deduction upon the swish of a gown allied to patently male steps. But listen to those steps themselves, Watson. They are not made by the soft shoe of an oriental potentate; rather they are like the sound made by Dutch clogs. However, there is a sharp click to the step, as if from raised heel and toe. I believe we are to expect a member of some monastic order.'

I secretly thought that he could be wrong in this deduction and that we might be about to meet a woman with a deceptively determined step, or perhaps even, unlikely as it might seem in London on a fine evening, a Lancashire mill worker in a weatherproof cape. It would be nice, I felt, for my friend not to be correct for just this one instance. But alas, it was not to be.

'There is a Mr Septimus Culthorpe to see you, Mr Holmes. Although he has no appointment I let him in because, well because he is some kind of a priest.' She lowered her voice as she uttered the last few words, almost as if there were some disgrace in them.

Holmes replied, 'Of course, Mrs Hudson, I'm sure you were right to let him in. Pray bid him enter.'

The figure that loomed through the door was tall, lugubrious and wearing a green monk's habit tied at the waist with a red cord. He shot us each a bird-like glance and then extended a hand for my friend to shake. He spoke with a hoarse, thin voice. 'Mr Sherlock Holmes, I believe. Although I have never seen you before, I know you to be clean shaven.'

Holmes chuckled softly. 'Mr Culthorpe, you are a man after my own heart, and you are correct for my colleague is Dr John Watson.'

Culthorpe shook hands with me in turn and said, 'I have heard of you too, sir, and I would be most grateful if you would remain present when I tell Mr Holmes my story.'

This was rather amusing in a way, for the most usual

scenario at this point would have been for Holmes to introduce me and then say, 'This is my friend and colleague before whom you may speak freely.' Some hidden playwright appeared to be giving all the lines to this unusual visitor.

Holmes pulled a chair up to the fire so that Culthorpe sat between us, getting the benefit of the heat. He extended his claw-like hands, saying, 'It is a fine evening, but chilly. My blood has become thin through the Spartan existence of a monk.'

Holmes felt that it was his turn to speak a few telling lines. 'But I'll wager at least that you do not have the callused knees of the common or garden friar. I perceive that your order is not a religious one, neither is it silent but is, largely speaking, closed.'

The monk started slightly, then began to realize how these deductions had been made. 'You are right on all counts, my dear sir. I wear no cross or other pious emblem and my speech does not have the hesitance you might expect from one long forbidden converse. And my complexion is that of one who seldom leaves a monastic surrounding.'

Holmes applauded ironically. 'A man after our own heart, Watson! Now Mr Culthorpe, what does such a shrewd man as yourself think that he could require the services of Sherlock Holmes for?'

Culthorpe treated us to an acidic smile. 'It is a long story, Mr Holmes, but in the need to be thorough I fear I must risk boring you . . .'

Holmes took his hunter from his waistcoat pocket, studied it and said, 'See if you can tell it all in, shall we say, eight minutes? Cut all the corners, yet leave out nothing that is vital.'

'I will try, and I trust you both to interrupt me if I do not clarify each point. Well, I must begin at the beginning . . .'

We offered him tobacco and liquid refreshment but he waved these offerings away, commencing to speak in his very distinctive voice. 'Some few years ago I became dissatisfied with my style of living in this troublesome world. I was tempted to join a monastic order but had no religious faith. To cut a long story short I decided to start an order of my own which I called the Secret Seven, seven being a mysterious number, and I decided that it should be made up of just seven monks at any one time. I would choose the other six persons myself in the first instance and then, should any one of them die or leave for some reason, the rest of us would between us choose a member to replace him and bring the number back to the required number. My idea was that no one could apply to join, membership being by invitation only. Outside of the Vatican it would be the most exclusive of all monastic orders. It was to be entirely inter-denominational, indeed persons without religious faith could be included. We have even had an atheist among our number. Several of the present seven are agnostic, and there are no services of any kind. We give our lives to contemplation, discussion, debate and each of the seven has a definite occupation to help with our self-supporting nature. We keep goats for milk and cheese, grow our own fruit and vegetables, and have a large pond from which we take a few carp. We do not beg, borrow or steal . . .' Eloquent, he paused for the first time.

I took pity on him, feeling that a question would give him a chance to draw breath. 'Mr Culthorpe, where is this monastery in which the seven of you reside?'

'Ah, Dr Watson, a shrewd question. You wonder perhaps where the finance comes from for us to lead this idyllic life; for although we are self-supporting in most things there would be the matter of rent. Well, although not a rich man I am the owner of a large old house deep in the country which is where the Secret Seven reside, rent free.'

Holmes had a question too. 'Rent free or no, Mr Culthorpe, there is no such thing as being completely and utterly self-supporting. Are your members, then, of independent means?'

'Not all of them; some are chosen on account of their previous occupation. We make our own wine and sell a little of it, or trade it for flour and other stable commodities.'

Holmes again studied his hunter. 'Mr Culthorpe, I have found this recitation of yours regarding the Secret Seven to be of interest; but we did say eight minutes, did we not? That leaves just three minutes for you to tell us why you are informing Sherlock Holmes about your fascinating association.'

I had found Culthorpe's oration of great interest, but I could understand why someone of Holmes's disposition perhaps wondering just why this rather bizarre man had called to tell us about his extraordinary way of life.

Septimus Culthorpe sat forward in his chair and spoke with more urgency in his voice. 'Mr Holmes, Dr Watson, forgive me if I have dwelt upon the details of my idyll. I will get straight to the point of my urgent need of your help. All went as I had planned it for the first few years of the establishment of the Secret Seven, until just a week or two ago when one of our number died, suddenly, and since then a second member of our order has expired as well. Two of them within twenty days; this makes it necessary for me to find two fresh faces for our group.'

Holmes had looked up with fresh interest at the mention of the deaths, but still had impatience in his voice. 'Whilst accepting that two such deaths within such a short time is unusual it hardly has a sinister ring to it. I am assuming that both were somewhat elderly and that you have found no obviously sinister circumstances; come sir, you have illustrated to us your own shrewdness and would have recognized any signs of foul play.'

Culthorpe looked troubled as he replied, 'Mr Holmes, both of the deceased brethren were less than fifty years old. One of them three and forty and the other nine and forty. Indeed we have *none among us* to be considered as elderly. What is more, both of them appeared to have received some kind of threat or warning, of which they would not speak.'

Holmes was now more attentive, and asked, 'These warnings, as you call them: do you think them to have been written or orally delivered?'

'Oh written, for it could be no coincidence surely that both of these unfortunates received a letter just a day or so before their demise.'

'Is it unusual for your members to receive postal communications?'

'Oh yes, very. You see all of them have chosen to retire

from the troubles of this world ; indeed most have not even informed friends or relatives of their whereabouts. After all, it is the incursions of everyday life that have made them accept my invitation. None of them is hiding as a wanted criminal might be and all are anxious to be left in peace.'

I could see that Holmes was not convinced as yet that there was a situation present which called for his intervention. He said, 'But it is not inconceivable that coincidence could have delivered postal items to these two late lamented lay friars?'

Our visitor shifted in his seat, uncomfortable, not with the armchair we had provided but perhaps with the wisdom of speaking his next words. At length he had resolved his inner debate. 'Forgive my hesitance, a last-minute struggle with my own self concerning the wisdom of my next words. The letters that they received, in each case produced a profound effect upon their recipients, and both were contained in exactly similar envelopes and sealed with red wax.'

My friend was interested now, his manner becoming more probing. One could almost say he rapped out his question. 'You have these letters and their envelopes?'

'Alas no, they could not be found following the two unfortunate deaths. I admit that I made no great attempt to find the first, but for the second one I liberally searched. Then when yesterday morning this third similar envelope arrived for brother Campion I realized that I had to . . .'

Holmes interrupted him. 'You say a third envelope has been received by one of your number; it is exactly similar to the other two and sealed with red wax?'

'Yes . . .'

'What was the reaction of this brother Campion when he opened and read the letter it contained?'

'He betrayed surprise at first, yet did not start or show the obvious concern as did the other two.'

'Did you not enquire of him concerning the nature of the letter?'

'I have sworn that I will not concern myself with the private affairs of any brother. After all, these men have accepted my invitation to join our circle with such privacy in mind.'

Holmes refilled his pipe and lit it with a vesta. He did this in his usual unhurried style despite his rising interest in the problems of Septimus Culthorpe. Eventually he spoke. 'I understand, sir, your predicament; you cannot even consult the police without breaking your word to your people. What, by the way, were the officially recognized causes of death of your two deceased brethren?'

'Both died of heart failure, presumably during sleep.'

'The third, the one who has so recently received the letter, does he appear to be in good health?'

'Certainly, he is a man in the prime of life and although his manner has somewhat quietened he has made no allusion to the letter or any sort of problem.'

'What shall you do by the way concerning the replacement of the two that have died?'

'I have as yet postponed all thought concerning that matter. If nothing else untoward occurs for a reasonable length of time I will be looking around for suitable candidates. I am hoping that no journalist gets onto this matter lest he spoil our restful privacy.'

Holmes was very thoughtful in expression and movements before he again spoke. When he did it was at some length, and what he had to say presented to me a bombshell. 'Mr Septimus Culthorpe, you have brought me a very real problem and you are quite right to do so, given your difficulty with the privacy that you have promised your brethren and in any case having no obvious crime to lay before the police. But I am intrigued enough by the circumstances and bizarre nature of these deaths (also I am concerned for the third recipient of a communication) to be willing to give the whole matter my undivided attention. I cannot very well visit your retreat either in my own persona or in some pretended one, unless . . .'

Culthorpe and I hung upon his words and I could see that some ingenious thought had entered his mind. He continued, 'Unless I become a chosen member of your order. Better still, Watson and I fill, temporarily of course, the two missing members needed to bring the Secret Seven back to its full strength, and perhaps helping prevent a third tragedy.'

Culthorpe started and then his face wreathed in a broad smile. 'Oh Mr Holmes, what a splendid idea! Why then you could be right on the spot, and I could confer with you frequently in private, for as initiates you would need such conference and it would not be unusual. Of course, you would need to find definite occupations to follow. The two that we have lost were an apiarist and a weaver. But we do not have a physician.'

Holmes smiled wickedly as he caught my eye. 'Well there you are, my dear Watson. Your wife will be quite amazed to return from the antipodes to learn that you have not only taken to the celibate life of a monk, but a healer too!'

I was a little taken aback by it all. 'I say, look here, Holmes, I feel we need to discuss this . . .'

He cut me short. 'Nothing to discuss, my dear fellow. You said you were free to stay with me for the next few weeks; well, stay with me you shall, and the quiet of a monastery will do your shattered city nerves a power of good. As for myself, I look forward to taking up some new occupation, whilst secretly pursuing my own. I cannot think that I could become a weaver, but the management of an apiary intrigues me. I have several books upon bee-keeping in my tattered collection. One acquires these tomes without the thought that they might come in useful.'

In the fullness of time, of course, I would find this introduction to bees to be prophetic as far as Sherlock Holmes was concerned. But at that time I doubt that the thought of the production of honey as more than mere excuse for his intended presence at the monastery.

As Culthorpe prepared to leave, a far happier man than he had been when he arrived at 221B, he arranged that we would arrive at Grimstone Priory upon the morrow. 'I will collect you at the railway station at twelve midday; I have a dogcart which is capital for the purpose. Please bring a minimum of baggage.'

As he left, I breathed long and hard as I rounded upon Sherlock Holmes, chastising him verbally for arranging a matter quite above my head, that I would have preferred to omit from my itinerary altogether. 'Really, Holmes, it is unworthy of you to make these arrangements in such a manner that I could hardly extricate myself from them, at least in front of Mr Culthorpe!'

His manner was placating. 'Dear old friend, who else could I turn to at such a moment of need, especially when circumstances have made your involvement seem almost decreed by fate. You came to stay with me and my expedition required two persons. 'Tis kismet, Watson; it was meant to be.'

It took perhaps an hour before I became completely resigned to what had been arranged. I argued increasingly without conviction that I should not be party to this undertaking. But Holmes in turn cajoled, threatened, coaxed and demanded. 'To begin with, Watson, there is no one else that I can depend upon to assist me with this matter. I will, if the matter is as serious as I suspect it might be, need at my side a man with a keen mind and quick reactions. Also I need someone who can slip into the role selected for him. Who better than a doctor to impersonate a physician? You can say that you are a herbalist if it offends your medical ethics. Your role is the easier of the two, for someone of your experience. Although we may take very little luggage I must certainly take my books on bee-keeping as part of mine. I will study them whilst we are on the train, then at least I will be able to talk with some intelligence upon the subject of apiary.'

I was finally resigned to my role. 'Where is this Grimstone Priory?'

'It is near the village of Grimstone, in Sussex, not far from Fowlhaven.'

I was still not much better informed. 'I don't even know Fowlhaven, let alone Grimstone.'

'Oh, it is fairly close to Eastbourne; there is a stopping train from Charing Cross which stops at Grimstone according to Culthorpe, and arrives there at about midday. But I will make sure that this is indeed so.'

He busied himself with the timetable whilst I fumed, though perhaps a little less fiercely. Then I took up the map of Sussex and studied it. The Priory was actually marked upon the map, not far from a village called Middle Dicker. There was a stream marked Cuckmere, and the nearest actual town appeared to be Hailsham. It was a part of Sussex with which I was not completely familiar, yet I could see from the map that the Priory was extremely isolated. The nearest railway station appeared to be Uckfield, which Holmes assured me was our train destination for the morrow.

I packed a few things in a small gladstone. A razor, a toothbrush, a change of linen and my service revolver! Holmes insisted that we needed no change of clothes as we would soon be wearing green habits with red cord belts. I confess that I was not looking forward to any of it.

I tried to rise early upon the following morning but old habits die hard despite the best regulated repeater clock. Then I tucked into my breakfast like the fat boy in the *Pickwick Papers* before I spoke a word to the irritatingly shaven, fed and calm Sherlock Holmes. As I gulped my coffee I said, 'Surely there is no rush, Holmes? I believe the train leaves at ten and three quarters.'

Holmes consulted his hunter and said, 'I dislike being rushed, Watson, as you well know.'

I well knew nothing of the sort, knowing him to be a past master at leaving things to the last minute and usually revelling in the art of doing everything by the skin of his teeth as far as punctuality was concerned. He had already skimmed through *The Thundererer*, but suggested that he would need plenty of time to ensure the purchase of other newspapers at the station bookstall.

'After all, Watson, we will be cut off from civilization for perhaps several weeks. I must indulge myself in reading all the broadsheets whilst we are on the train.'

I all but snapped, 'I thought you were going to study bee-keeping upon the journey?'

It was his soft answer which turned away my wrath. 'I spent several hours studying *The Apiarist's Handbook* and *Practical Bee Keeping* whilst you were safely in the arms of Morphus. Did you know, Watson, it all depends upon the queen. The workers and drones and other menial bees do everything required for the making of the honey. She sits there safely in her hive, rather like my brother Mycroft who does it all from the Diogenes Club!'

Despite my previous ill-humour I was forced to laugh at his rather clever bit of comparison.

At all but exactly ten of the clock Billy knocked, entered, and announced, "Ansom for Mr Holmes and the Doctor. . . . I let two go, and then grabbed this 'un!'

There was time only for the shortest of farewells to Mrs Hudson and, once again, Sherlock Holmes and I were off on yet another great adventure. I had shared so many of his exploits and however dangerous they might be at the time I had grown to accept them in the spirit of a third person looking at the two of us from a hide. Often, as when we evaded the great Grypon Mire I had caught myself saying, 'What fools these mortals be!'

CHAPTER 2

Grimstone Priory

The station was little more than a halt, with two raised wooden platforms, one on each side of the lines. But there were no buildings of any kind save for a signal box in the near distance. The Sussex downs were to the south of us, but in the other direction there was a rare (for Sussex) expanse of flat country. One very distant but obviously very large building could be clearly seen, standing perhaps two to three miles to the north-east of us which we both suspected must be Grimstone Priory. There was a track, rather than a road, which seemed to lead in that general direction and before long we spied a cloud of dust which eventually proved to be a horse-drawn vehicle, which became clearer by the second. Then within four or five minutes we could make out the general shape of a dogcart pulled by a grey, and within another couple of minutes more we could vaguely make out the shape of a girdled friar who appeared to be driving it.

Holmes eventually said, 'I believe our host approaches,

Watson, and I hope you have brought a bandanna to tie around your face, for I perceive that the grey kicks up quite a dust storm. There must have been less rain here than in the metropolis.

'Gentlemen, my apologies for your wait; the train was obviously early for perhaps the first time that I can remember. Pray pile in to the dogcart, kick the spaniel to one side if she bothers you.'

We greeted Culthorpe politely, and climbed into the vehicle, but ignoring his invitation to kick the dog. I am fond of canines and although Holmes is not there is nothing sadistic in his character. He carefully avoided the slavering soft mouth, whilst I patted the quivering little bitch and admired her compact beauty. She had those spaniel sad eyes and jowls, giving her a look of extreme sadness even when perfectly serene.

Holmes spoke. 'I cannot quite understand why you did not stay in London overnight and travel down with us, Culthorpe.'

I thought I caught a slightly evasive note in the reply. 'Why, having definitely arranged for you to come to the Priory I needed to make some arrangements for your reception.'

I thought I should speak. 'I trust you have not put yourself out in that respect, sir. Indeed, the less fuss is made of us the easier will be our task.'

Holmes nodded, grunted and fussed with his pipe, eventually saying, 'Although Sussex is a fairly highly populated county, one could well be in the Scottish lowlands or even parts of Dartmoor; though the soil is largely of chalk which produces a scarring which one seldom sees elsewhere. You realize, Watson, that this whole county was once under the sea. But that cruel ocean gives nothing away; in return for rendering to us that which you see it has taken as much back into the bosom of the deep. There are entire towns far under the English Channel. The gorse which grows so well in chalk is largely worthless save in that it attracts the honey bee.'

Culthorpe chuckled drily, 'Ah, so you have already made a start in the study of the bee. Splendid, Holmes, we will make an apiarist of you in no time at all. We will shortly be passing the hives, on your right. But from here you can already see something of Grimstone Priory; built of local stones and flints in medieval times, burnt to the ground by Henry the Eighth and restored in the reign of good Queen Bess. It has been in my family since its restoration. But as I have no descendants I decided to form the association of which you have learned.'

I peered at the looming grey shape and noted that it appeared to be of two castle-like structures, bridged by a lower strung building between. I imagined that at one time there might have been four turrets, only two of which had been restored, with a quadrant inside the outer walls. I vividly imagined the lord of the manor within this walled area, ruling over what must have been like a tiny enclosed village. Perhaps even before a stone edifice was first erected there was a vast timber building which had been defended by yeoman British against Saxons, Danes and Normans in turn.

Ever practical, Holmes inquired, 'In what hands was

Grimstone Priory at the time when bluff King Hal destroyed it?'

'It was a monastery, with Franciscan Friars, so you see if you discount the religious aspect, the wheel has made a full turn.'

I asked a practical question. 'What shall we be called within your Priory, surely not Holmes and Watson?'

Culthorpe replied, 'Did I not mention that none of us uses his given name within our walls? We are named after our trade or occupation. I suggest Dr Watson that you be called Brother Healer and your colleague could be Brother Hive. These were the names by which your unfortunate predecessors were known.'

Soon we passed the hives, and then we were at that grim grey Grimstone Priory itself. We could see that when built in Elizabethan times it would have been considered old fashioned, constructed as it was in imitation of the original monastery. The sharp flints that had been effectively spaced among the more usual grey stones saved the edifice from that stark appearance of so many castles and monastic buildings. There were no glass windows, just apertures, some of the higher ones being mere slits through which arrows could have been shot. The flat tops of both towers were surrounded by low serrated stone walls. One could very easily imagine a lookout patrol atop of each.

We drove through a gateway which had not had its gates closed for months, if not years, according to Holmes. He explained, 'You will notice how well established are the convolvulus which have climbed and entwined themselves around the gates' rails. Their roots would have been destroyed had the gates been opened. But I admire your Brother Gardener for leaving them. They are attractive, are they not? Oh I know they are considered to be weeds that will choke other plants which are not; but who is to say that they are not more effective than that which they destroy, Beauty is indeed in the eye of the beholder.'

The wheels of the dogcart ground upon the shingled path up to the entrance to the priory and a jolly fat friar, or a personage of that appearance, ran out to greet us. We were introduced as Brother Hive and Brother Healer, to Brother Pisces who evidently tended the fishpond. He greeted us warmly in a broad south country accent, saying, 'Come, we are back to seven again! I will cook stuffed carp to celebrate, assuming that I can catch the sly old codgers. Some of them are a hundred years old you know!'

I secretly hoped that he might hook a couple of middle-aged fish rather than the centenarians which I considered might be a bit leathery.

Holmes held up his bag with only his little finger crooked under its handle. He said, 'How delightful to have luggage of a featherweight nature; gives one a grand feeling of freedom.'

We were shown to our cells as two quite adequate apartments were referred to. Each had a cot, a rough-hewn chair and a table also made by a journeyman carpenter; perhaps one of the monks. One quickly got used to having no glass in the apertures which served as windows; there was a screen with three folds which could be placed around the cot to keep out draughts. It was one of those objects popular when the Queen was young, its thin wood surface covered with shiny printed scraps.

Far from being of a religious theme these were of musical comedy star beauties, cats, birds, flowers and other flora and fauna, all a little scratched and faded but charming none the less. I mentioned it to Holmes who told me that he too had a screen but that his was covered with Chinese wallpaper of a rather more recent fashion fad. He looked very strange to me in his green habit, but then I probably looked far more bizarre in my friar's garb. It took me a long time to get used to the footwear and absence of hosiery!

We were both looking at the screen in Holmes's cell when Septimus Culthorpe joined us, having first struck upon the floor, outside the apartment, three times with his staff, rather in the manner of the stage manager of a Parisian music hall. Holmes bade him enter.

'Brother Hive, and Brother Healer too. I hope you are both settling in well? I see you are admiring the late brother's screen It was about the only intrinsic thing that he brought here with him. Of course we have screens here, but of a rather less festive nature such as the one in your own cell, Brother Healer.'

Holmes asked, 'Do you imagine, Brother Septimus, that these scraps indicate the late bee-keeper's interests or that he merely used them for decorative purposes? I notice that some are quite recently applied and others have been where they are for a considerable number of years.'

I asked, 'How can you tell that all the scraps were not stored for many years and then used to decorate the screen in a single operation?'

He answered, 'I am basing my assessment on the age of

the varnish that has been applied rather than the scraps themselves. If you look carefully you will see that the shade and condition of the varnish varies. Moreover, there are some items which have not been varnished at all, though probably the intention to eventually apply it was there. This simply means that his collection of these items was a continuing interest. Let us repair to Watson's cell and look at his screen.'

We did as Holmes suggested and he examined the faded Chinese wallpaper carefully. Very gently he pulled back some of that which was peeling from the screen. As he did this a number of paper squares of various sizes fluttered to the ground. We picked these up and placed them upon the rude table. Some of these were of the kind that one might have expected; for example, a birth certificate, a military discharge document and things of such a nature. But one of the papers appeared to be quite new in appearance. Holmes lifted this and examined it carefully, saying, 'It is addressed to one Gerald Carter. Was this the name of the late occupant of this room? I imagine so, for the name matches that on the birth certificate.'

Culthorpe nodded and said, 'Yes, and of course as you know he was one of the now-deceased brethren.'

Holmes said, 'I believe we now have one of the mysterious communications which arrived in envelopes with the red seal. I could wish that we also had the envelope, but must make the most of the letter itself.' He spread the epistle upon the table and I noted that it was written in a rather spidery style, probably with a quill.

Box: 427. Harmon and Grant Ltd., 269 Commercial Street, London E.

Dear Sir,

Please write to me at the above address if you wish to hear of something to your advantage. I enclose a postage stamp for your use in case it is difficult for you to obtain one in your present situation.

Yours faithfully,

J.D. Norton.

I pointed at a discoloration on the paper with a forefinger and said, 'I assume that is a scrap of adhesive from the stamp which was attached for his use.'

Holmes waved my finger aside and chided me, 'Do not touch it, Watson. It may be of most singular interest but I would value your impression of the letter.'

I said, 'There is of course this address in Commercial Street. I imagine you will be wanting to make contact in that direction?'

Holmes shook his head. 'I noticed at once that it was a false address. No such number exists in Commercial Street, and one can also therefore assume that J.D. Norton is equally fictitious.'

Culthorpe asked, 'How about the handwriting, does that tell you anything?'

Holmes shrugged. 'Only that the writer was a man, perhaps middle aged, yet rather old fashioned and set in his ways. By the way, he was left handed and of a rather impatient nature.'

Septimus Culthorpe nodded admiringly. 'I can see that you are right in that it is a man's writing, and the direction of the writing suggests that he was left handed, but I cannot quite see how you have defined his nature or his age.'

I said, 'I can appreciate that he is old fashioned in that he still uses a quill in this day and age of steel nibs.'

'Quite so, Watson, and his writing is firm with no sign of that slight hesitance of style which age seems to bring. But you will notice that of some ten "i's" he has dotted only three of them: a sign of impatience.'

'But if his name and address are both false why on earth did he want those to whom he wrote to reply to them?'

'Watson, these replies which he suggested interested him not at all, obviously it was the very action of making a reply that interested him. Where is the nearest posting box, Culthorpe?'

'About a mile in the direction of the village.'

Culthorpe left us, with the suggestion that a simple meal would be ready within the hour. Holmes decided to use that time in taking a walk, during which we would inspect the place where the return letters had been posted, after we had changed into our monkish garb. I did not relish such an early test of my ability to face the world as a brother, but Holmes insisted. 'Come, Watson, we are deep in the country, we will meet few people and those that we do meet will doubtless be used to the presence of the Secret Seven. Let us plunge in at the deep end.'

As we walked the path beside the railway line, which we were assured would lead us to our goal, I tried to get used to the robe and wooden shoes. I felt sure that I created a bizarre picture, yet had to admit that my friend quite looked the part. The robe seemed to suit his ascetic appearance, and the extra height given by the shoes made him of impressive height. We both carried staffs, which I assumed were ritualistic rather than practical. Doubtless brethren of times gone by had needed to ward off attacks by footpads or even wolves.

We found the postbox, a neat rectangular metal box, painted red and bearing the usual V.R. crest. It was not a full-sized postbox of the kind to be found in towns, rather made to be attached to a wall as was this one. It was in fact fixed to the outside of a tiny shop of a sort so fast disappearing.

'Good afternoon, good sir!' I greeted the shopkeeper with what I imagined to be the right mixture of respect and reverence.

But Holmes glared at me and, as usual, he showed me how to do it. 'Greetings, brother provider. Have you amongst your provender a brand of tobacco known as Scottish Mixture?'

'Why yes, brother, here you are.'

The transaction over, Holmes started upon the pleasantries of small talk, yet with a calculating gleam in his eye. 'We are the new brethren at the Priory, just learning our way about. I'll wager you knew the two brothers that we have replaced?'

'Oh yes, I knew them well. Usually they were full of fun and out for a good gossip, both of them. Yet strangely the last I saw of either of them was when they used the postbox. In both instances they seemed rather off colour, just slipping their letters in the box and turning straight back toward the Priory. I remarked to the wife only yesterday how strange that they both died so suddenly, and both so soon after using the postbox which they had neither of them used before.'

Holmes looked skywards, placed his hands together and said, 'Well, the Lord is our shepherd and we are his sheep. Certainly it was a strange coincidence, especially when you say that they both appeared unwell.'

The shopkeeper said, 'After the second brother died I wondered if there was some sort of infection up at the Priory; but time has passed and all seems well up there, so I don't think you need to worry.'

As we walked back we mused upon the strange coincidence of the demise of the two brothers who had evidently only in common the receiving of similar letters and using the same postbox in order to make reply.

Holmes said, 'I do not believe the shared postbox is of any significance. I have no doubt that if one walked as far in the opposite direction one would find such a box. That both of the deceased made reply is of more import; and why would they not when confronted with the hint of monetary gain? Yet the false name and address shows that their replies were of no value. Very strange, Watson, very strange indeed.'

I could make no reply that would have served any purpose: I too found it all very strange.

At the big scrubbed top table we were treated to a simple, wholesome meal of bread, cheese, mutton and broth.

This we washed down with tankards of home-made wine, which was excellent. We were introduced by Culthorpe to the four brothers who completed the company. Brother Shepherd, whose occupation was obvious, proved to be a round-faced friar whose crucifix showed that he was one of only two religious brethren. The other, Brother Reaper, also wore a crucifix, but was of a different and rather more simplistic Christian faith. Both were rubicund of face and figure, in direct contrast to Brother Carp, a tall lean man who had charge of the fish pond. There remained Brother Abacus who was in charge of the financial welfare of the priory. He was a short, fussy-looking man with an irritating habit of drumming his fingers upon the table. He was a little abrasive, but the other three were pleasant enough.

Brother Shepherd said, 'I think you are both very brave to be joining us at such a time. Both the late brothers received letters in similar envelopes sealed with red wax. I have not spoken of it before, but I can tell you now that I have myself received such a letter.'

Holmes decided not to declare his interest by voice or deed, asking quietly, 'You replied to it?'

Shepherd said, 'No, I did not, I am not superstitious, Brother Hive, but after what had happened I took no chances and threw it into the fire.'

Later, when the four of them had retired, we sat and took a last pipe with Culthorpe, who as soon as it was safe to talk said, 'My lips were sealed, as you know; but I am delighted that Brother Shepherd volunteered that which I could not ask him. What is your reaction to his words, Holmes?'

Holmes replied, 'I am horrified and delighted all at once,

my dear Culthorpe. I am horrified that he has destroyed something which could have provided valuable aid to our investigation, but of course one must be delighted that his life is probably not in danger due to his action.'

I said, 'But Holmes, the chances are that the letter to Shepherd would have been identical to the one we have seen.'

'Just as lethal too, Watson, had he not burned it.'

Culthorpe decided to retire and after a further five minutes I did the same, sensing that Holmes wished to ponder the problem on his own, a two- or three-pipe problem.

I slept fitfully, my dreams full of huge red seals and monks clutching deadly missives in shaking hands. These fearful figments of my slumbering imagination were as nothing compared to the shock and horror that the dreadful clanging rising bell produced. I sat bolt upright upon my primitive cot and there was Sherlock Holmes in a state of great excitement attempting to tell me something which my soporific brain could not seem to take in. I said, 'Holmes, I was fast asleep, so pray start again to tell me that which you wish to impart.'

He was impatient. 'Upon my word, Watson, you spend half your life in sleep and the other half in some sort of dreamlike existence. Listen to me while I tell you that I believe I have solved the mystery of the two dead friars.'

I was wide awake now and struggling into my habit, yet I poured ice cold water from the wash basin over my face and hands to ensure that I had heard him right. I demanded, 'Tell me again, Holmes, for I am now quite alert.'

Had it been politic for him to shout he would have done so. 'As I sat pondering upon the enigma I had spread the letter, the only one of the three that we have, upon the floor before me. As I sat back in my chair, enjoying a pipe, I noticed a mouse darting about the floor.'

I knew that Holmes did not share my own dread of rats and mice so I was a little surprised to hear him make anything of the rodent's presence. I said, 'Come, although we rarely see a mouse at Baker Street they are rather to be expected in such an old building as this.'

'True, Watson, and I gave it little thought, save when at one moment it was healthy and lively, yet the next stone dead.' Unusual as this might sound I still could not fathom why Holmes had burst in upon me to tell me about it in such a wildly excited fashion and said as much, but his answer explained the singularity.

'Watson, a live, healthy, alert mouse settled upon the letter which was spread near the hearth, then within seconds it was stone dead. I examined it carefully, and found all the symptoms of poisoning.'

I tried to apply logic. 'Perhaps the creature had taken poison that had been placed down with the very purpose of its destruction?'

'I doubt it, for most poisons designed for such a purpose will cause the animal to seek water or at least the open air. This one was behaving quite normally until seconds after it had settled upon the letter. Something upon that paper probably killed it.'

Then to my horror he produced the dead mouse, wrapped in a handkerchief from within his robe. Obviously he wished me to examine it, which I did, although with no sort of enjoyment.

I had to admit that the creature exhibited every symptom of having been destroyed by a deadly poison. I applied my nose as close as I could to the animal, short of touching it and said, 'Bitter almonds, Holmes; cyanide I fancy. You are right, for if it had taken cyanide elsewhere it would have dropped within seconds. But what could have been upon that letter to effect such a drastic demise even of such a tiny creature?'

Holmes took the letter from his robe and passed it to me. 'Give this the same test as you did the late rodent.'

I passed the letter beneath my nostrils and detected that same bitter sweet odour. 'Could it be the ink that is contaminated?'

'I think not. I believe it is that mere trace of gum from the stamp which was attached by its corner that is responsible for the death of the mouse.'

It was logical enough: the killer sending the victim a stamp, seemingly as a matter of courtesy for his reply. He had treated the gummed back with cyanide and then attached it to the letter by one corner which he had doubtless dampened with a brush or pad rather than with his tongue. The non-existent address was logical too for the object was to destroy whoever received the letter and not to receive a reply. The cyanide was powerful enough to kill whoever applied his tongue to the gum. The trace on the paper would have been minute, yet strong enough to destroy a mouse. I remarked, 'The two deaths were definitely not from natural causes, so do you think we should make application for the unfortunate monks to be exhumed?'

Holmes shook his head. 'I think not, Watson, for we

already know that they were poisoned, little purpose would be served. But we must be alert now in the knowledge that we are dealing with an ingenious and ruthless killer whose motives are as yet beyond our understanding and made more so by the lack of any connection between the two victims and the intended one, save a desire to live a quiet life of contemplation. Our task is twofold, Watson: to discover a motive whilst trying to protect the surviving brethren from a similar fate. If the perpetrator of these crimes is ignorant of our involvement he may try the same fiendish trick again, but if he tries a completely fresh set of tactics we may be looking for someone closer to the heart of the matter.'

'You mean the criminal could be one of the brethren?' Such a thought appalled me but I had to allow it to enter my mind.

Holmes remarked, thoughtfully, 'The possibility seems unlikely, but we cannot discount it, Watson; no, we cannot discount it entirely!'

'In which case we should keep your discovery from all save Culthorpe?'

'For the moment, from all, including Culthorpe.'

CHAPTER 3

The Five Suspects

As we sat with our brethren around the breakfast table Holmes enquired of Culthorpe if there were any letters that had been delivered. He asked the question quite openly for all to hear. Culthorpe shook his head.

'None, Brother Hive, and this is not unusual for are we not all here that we might withdraw from the troubles of this world? It is rare for a brother to receive a letter and therefore we seldom see the postman. By the way, Brother Campion will take you to your apiary and give you some instruction. Brother Healer, you might care to join them for today, unless anyone should need your services?'

He glanced around enquiringly but all present shook their heads. Evidently there were no sprains, headaches, cuts or bruises; at least for that moment.

It was good to be out among the hives despite my apprehension concerning the bees themselves. Whilst Campion was otherwise engaged I asked Holmes, as quietly as I could manage, 'Why do you suppose Culthorpe seemed to go out of his way to give the brother who guides us his real name, Campion? This after making so much of referring to everyone by his occupational title?'

'I had also wondered at this, Watson, but we must note it as something possibly trivial and yet possibly not.'

Brother Campion, or rather Brother Shepherd as we had learned to call him, showed us the row of hives and directed Holmes how to lift out the slides wherein lay the honeycombs. I was unnerved by the large number of bees that were brought up with each slide.

Shepherd said, 'The bulk of the bees are swarming, but there are always a few to be found here. Handle the slides with care; they will only sting if you make any unusually frantic movement.'

I was amazed at how Holmes seemed to take to the care of the hives and collection of the honey, being rarely stung and only then because he tended to forsake the use of the gloves and hood provided.

When I chided him for this he said, 'Brother Healer, you should know how often I have injected myself with needles far more formidable than the sting of a bee!'

After the care of the hives had been completed, Shepherd suggested that we might like to join him in the meadow where his flock were to be found. This we did willingly, at least as far as I was concerned for I have always found sheep to be particularly pleasant animals and their bleating to be very soothing to the ear. Brother Shepherd showed us how he needed no sheepdog to control his flock through the presence of a goat to lead them.

'They will follow him as they would a ram, but he is

more intelligent and I have trained him to follow my calls.'

When we had aided him with the distribution of fodder and water for his flock we sat down in the meadow and took refreshment; cheese, bread and flasks of cider from the Priory apples. Shepherd told us his story without any prompting or questioning on our part, and I will give the reader a shortened version of the oration with which he intrigued us.

'I was born in Ingatestone, which is a small town in Kent. I went to a church school and my parents hoped that I would become a priest. But I had other ideas and wanted to try my luck as a trader. I bought some bales of cloth which I felt would make my fortune in Australia which was a growing market. I had a sweetheart, Eliza Doughty, with whom I had an understanding that I would either return to marry her within three years or else I would send her a ticket that she might join me in the antipodes. I wrote to her regularly and for the first year I received her answers. Afterwards she ceased to reply to my letters and at the end of three years I returned to England to find her and claim her hand. I had made, not a fortune, but enough money to open some sort of business. I assumed that some misunderstanding had caused her to cease writing to me. But when I got back to Ingatestone I learned that she had married a Londoner who had swept her off her feet and carried her off to the capital. After much painstaking enquiry I discovered the address in London to which she had removed, but imagine my dismay to find that she had been reduced to the level of the rascal himself who was a sneak-thief, confidence man and everything that was disgraceful.

I implored her to leave him and take up with me again, but he had ruined her to the extent that she eventually took her own life.

'When I learned of this I was at first just heartbroken, but then I became full of thoughts of revenge. So I confronted the fellow and started to set about him with my fists. He drew a knife on me but I managed to wrest it from him. The fight continued and unfortunately we fell to the ground in such a way that he was mortally injured, although I had harboured no wish other than to give him a hiding. I was of course arrested and charged with murder. Fortunately, however, the charge was reduced to one of unlawful killing, and the judge seemed to believe my story and gave me the shortest sentence that he could. Even so, I spent a number of years in prison. After my release I became a waster, soon spending my money in a number of sinful ways. Then, when I had struck rock bottom, I heard about this wonderful community. The rest is obvious to you; I have regained here my self-respect and my happiness has been marred only by the deaths of the two brethren. Ah well, you have heard enough of me; it is time the sheep were transferred to another pasture.'

We both took a liking to Brother Shepherd and were almost sorry when it was time for the three of us to return to the Priory. We knew the rules and needed not to be told that we should not repeat anything that Shepherd had told us in confidence. We had little way of knowing if he had been equally frank concerning his past with the other brothers, yet would later learn that we had been alone chosen for Shepherd's admissions.

'Well, Brother Hive, shall we be having honey with our fine hot baked bread?'

Culthorpe made this enquiry to which Holmes responded with considerable confidence. He said, 'Brother Prior, I feel sure that all will be well with the honey. I have no more than three or four stings, and the tobacco and other impurities in my system have made me immune.'

There was some laughter and I felt quite relaxed at the table despite the dangers that lurked and the ominous possibility of the very presence of our criminal tormentor. The meal was of stuffed carp, sage and thyme with onions, sewn into and cooked with the gigantic fish, from a recipe direct from Izaak Walton, or so Brother Pisces assured us. 'I tried to catch this fellow to celebrate your arrival yesterday but failed. However, today I was lucky and this fellow I estimate to be about five and seventy. They are at their best at that age.'

I was slightly puzzled. 'Brother Pisces, how can you be sure that this is the same fish that you angled for yesterday?'

His face wreathed in smiles. 'When you have been nurturing carp as long as I have, Brother Healer, you just know these things. This particular fish I have known for a number of years and have caught and returned him to the pond upon more than one occasion. One also knows when the time has come to make a meal of them in turn. We husband them with care, taking no more than to suit our modest requirements; that way they multiply just enough to supply our needs. It is not a lake, just a large pond, but carp are peculiar in that they breathe the oxygen in the water sparingly so that many fish can thrive in conditions that would soon kill off perch, roach, dace or pike. These would need the agitation of running water or at the least the space provided by a large lake. The carp is a splendid fellow: he can survive for an hour out of water. In China and Japan they have bred a dozen fancy varieties of gold and silver colour. The ingenious Orientals have also learned the secret of restricting the size to which they grow so that they can live their lifespan in bowls or glass tanks for decoration. They also miniaturize trees and shrubs with equally pleasing results.'

Holmes spoke the very words that were in my mind. 'I am amazed, with your obvious delight in them, that you can bear to catch and eat these creatures?'

Brother Pisces chuckled and said, 'So one would think, Brother, but when you consider that if I did not take a carp now and then they would soon die from lack of air and space. Even a carp can only survive in a certain degree of over-population. All I do is cull them so that they prosper; and we enjoy the fruits of this culling.'

Holmes enquired, 'How came you to have this interest in the well-being of fish, Brother Pisces?'

'Oh, I dwelt in this vicinity as a village child, angling in this very pond with string and bent pin when there was no one to see me off. That was in the old Squire's time. Then after some years as a wanderer I returned to this area and when Brother Culthorpe started this brotherhood I found it the perfect retreat for me, that I might lick the wounds that the world had inflicted upon me, and resume my great interest.'

The roasted stuffed carp was a really splendid meal; large enough for us all to eat our fill, washed down with a white wine which was also locally produced.

The only incident of note was when grace was about to be spoken by the two devout brothers. Holmes insisted upon placing a piece of the fish down for the cat. He explained this to the company.

'I am an agnostic, but I too have a code for living not dissimilar to that found in all versions of the good book. Yet I have a commandment of my own; "Thou shalt first feed one of nature's lowly creatures before thineself partaking". See how readily the good feline accepts my offering; this fills me with delight.'

The company were touched by his charming gesture, but as I had never seen him offer as much as a crumb of cheese to Mrs Hudson's cat I was not deceived. I realized that Holmes wished the cat to serve as a taster to ensure that there might be no repetition of death by poisoning! When the cat had eaten and shown no sign of distaste or distress for several minutes Holmes seemed happy for us all to partake of the carp. The good brothers were indeed so impressed with his gesture that at each meal one or other of them would offer the feline some of the fare. Holmes was happy with this but for reasons other than those that he had indicated.

Of course, Holmes could scarcely offer wine to the cat, but I noticed that he was always the first to taste it, taking a very small amount on his fingertip, explaining that this was his way when trying the quality of a vintage. This ruse also worked, for all would wait for his opinion upon the liquid refreshment assuming his expertise in wine tasting. Really, my friend's enterprise never ceased to amaze me.

Later, when we were alone, I congratulated Holmes upon his quick thinking at the dinner table. But his answer disappointed me.

'Watson, I never do anything upon the spur of the moment save in emergency. I had been evolving my scheme for having the food and drink tasted since our discovery of the poisoned stamp glue. As a medical man you will, I know, be ready to administer aid should I collapse following the fingertip testing of wine. In that manner I would take scarce a lethal dose. Should the cat keel over I imagine the brothers will have the good sense enough to forsake the food.'

I muttered, 'Enterprise thy name is Holmes . . . or rather Hive!'

That evening the brothers made merry, organizing some festivities to greet us. They sang merry songs accompanied by Brother Shepherd on a small organ, and Brother Chef, whose occupation was obvious both from his name and his appearance, treated us to a solo rendition of *Greensleeves* in a quite acceptable tenor voice. Then as things quietened down there were calls for some form of diversion from the two new brothers! My blood ran cold at the thought of having to recite, sing or perform a cakewalk. But I saved my face by telling Edgar Allan Poe's immortal story *The Black Cat*. Fortunately this was short and committed to my memory. As I finished there were cries of bravo and well told brother, and then their eyes were turned towards Holmes. I had no idea how he would handle this situation but of course I should have remembered how enterprising he could be. He had noticed an old violin in a corner, thick with dust but with its full complement of strings. There was a bow with it, although it had seen better days as indeed had the instrument itself. Holmes picked up the bow and the fiddle and cleaned them with his kerchief. Then he tuned the instrument and placed it to his chin. Of course I had heard Holmes play upon his own valuable antique violin many times, perhaps too many; but this wreck of a fiddle might prove to be a different matter.

'Is there anything in particular that you would like me to play?'

I thought that Holmes was over-playing his hand by offering to play a requested piece, but I need not have worried. They asked him for *The Blue Danube*, *Widdicombe Fair* and even for an Irish jig. To my amazement he managed all of these with verve and amazing execution. The brothers sat tapping their feet and clapping their hands and would not let him put down the violin until he had played many an encore. My surprise was occasioned by the fact that I had only ever heard Holmes play extremely obscure classical pieces, except when he drew wild notes from his own imagination.

During the days that followed, Holmes and I went our opposite ways, for I was set to help Brother Orchard whilst Holmes tended the bees. The care of the cider apples was interesting at first, but I found that Brother Orchard could be trying with his constant fount of knowledge concerning the fruit that he grew. But I followed his every word and tried to display awe-struck interest in the nurturing of pippins and brambles. Holmes had told me to observe everything that the brother said and did, for every friar was a suspect at that stage of our investigation. My friend had not ruled out the world at large, of course, but that was too large an area for us to sift without any lead as to direction.

I had made the mistake of questioning Holmes upon this very point of locality at first, and had received one of his more obscure replies. 'There is more light here, Watson!'

I confessed that his reply baffled me and this caused him to recite a parable.

'Watson, there was once a man who searched for that which he had dropped. He searched every room in his house without success. His wife was tired for the hour was late so she said, "Think, George, think, just where were you when you dropped it?" He replied, "I was out in the paddock." She asked, "Then why on earth are you searching for it in the house. Why don't you go and look in the paddock?" He said, "Because it is dark outside, there is more light here!"'

I thought I followed his train of thought, but could not be certain. However, fearing another parable I just nodded wisely. So we were looking for our suspect in the Priory because it was dark out in the great big world. Yet sooner or later, I considered, if no gleam of light fell upon that for which we searched, we might be forced into the great world again. The brothers all seemed to me to be beyond reproach: their company was well in its way, yet I yearned for a walk in Regent's Park, a night out at Drury Lane, a concert at the Royal Albert Hall, or just the sight and smell of Mrs Hudson's steak and kidney pudding.

It was upon the fourth day of our domicile that I managed to take on the errand of taking a cheese sandwich and a jar of cider to Holmes as he tended his hives.

Culthorpe had said to me, 'Watson, I appreciate that Holmes and yourself do not gain much opportunity to discuss my problem so I suggest that you do not return too quickly from your errand. After all, Brother Hive is expecting the return of his swarm and he may need your help.'

After carefully examining bread, cheese and cider we shared Holmes's repast and he handed me a piece of honeycomb, which was extremely pleasant so long as one made sure that no bees were loitering amid the sweetness.

'So Culthorpe suggested that you should come here upon the pretext of fetching my repast?'

'It was his suggestion, yes; he particularly inferred that we might want to discuss our findings without being overheard.'

'Do you think he believes that we have any findings to discuss?'

'I believe that he is hopeful that we may have.'

'Those findings that we have made, Watson, he is aware of already.'

'There is nothing else then?'

'Since last evening, nothing. I believe we discussed our progress to date.'

'But Holmes, surely you must have some thought in your

mind concerning the possible guilt of one or other of the brethren?'

Holmes pushed aside his bread and cheese and charged his clay, just as he might have done had we been at Baker Street. At length he spoke. 'There are five possible suspects at the Grange . . .'

I jumped in quickly. 'Only four. Surely you can discount Culthorpe? After all, he called your attention to this matter and engaged you to find the transgressor.'

He shook an admonishing pipe stem at me. 'At this stage I discount no one, or anything. Culthorpe might have engaged me in order to cloak his own guilt. Anyone, even an intelligent person, perhaps in a position of authority, might automatically believe in the innocence of someone like Culthorpe who himself drew attention to a tragic series of occurrences. But if you think back carefully you might remember that several times in my career I have been engaged to solve tragic mysteries which stemmed from the client himself. A certain type of transgressor will feel confident enough to play such a card. In saying this I do not mean that I am suspicious of Culthorpe; I just mention it as a possibility.'

I felt that the guilt of Culthorpe was more than unlikely, but did not want to lengthen an argument that I knew I could not win. So I tried another route to enlarging the possibilities.

'Accepting for the moment your view of Culthorpe, what are your feelings regarding the other four suspects?'

'I have thought carefully concerning each of them, Watson. I have tried to establish in my mind a motive for one or other of them. What advantage to any one of them to eliminate their brother friars, especially in light of Culthorpe's obvious determination to replace any who may fall by the wayside. Short of Culthorpe having made some kind of bizarre will which might favour a survivor one can see no motive. Had Brother Prior made such a will he would most certainly have informed me about it: remember, he is sharp of mind.'

I asked, 'Can we not then cast aside the matter of motive and consider them each from the point of view of character?'

He shrugged. 'Such an exercise might pass the time and could perhaps throw up some detail that could be useful to our enquiries. Who would you like to consider first?'

After some thought I asked, 'How about Brother Shepherd, or Campion as he was once known?'

'Ah yes, the man from the small Kentish village who returned from a business voyage to Australia to find that his sweetheart had been ruined by another whom he killed, albeit by accident. He is perhaps the only one of the four to have a criminal background yet I confess to finding him to be extremely honest in his manner and a very direct and decent man. Watson, my heart would direct me to consider him the least likely of the four to have possible connections with these crimes; yet my head must direct me, and my head has to take into account his criminal past.'

I thought this a good and fair assessment, coincidental with my own thoughts concerning Brother Shepherd.

Holmes continued, 'Now let us consider Brother Pisces. We know less of his background but one can tell that he is of good yeoman stock and his dialect suggests that he was born not far from where we are at this moment. His interest in fish in general, carp in particular, goes rather further than that of the mere angler. He told us of his boyhood interest and his return to his native pond after many years as a wanderer. We cannot ask him too many direct questions lest he suspect our motive, but I can tell that he has been a soldier, a coal miner and has possibly worked upon this estate long before Culthorpe's occupation.'

'How did you deduce that?'

'Oh, certain things that he has let drop in conversation have led me to believe that he has more knowledge of the Priory than his recent residence would account for.'

'You say that he has been a soldier?'

'He has a bearing and a way of cutting his hair quite unlike that of the other friars and suggests a military background.'

'. . . and a coal miner?'

'That was easily deduced from the way in which the coal dust has affected the pores of his skin. No amount of washing will remove every particle of the dust. I have also noticed that he can manage to move about in the Priory at dusk, even before the lamps are lit, with a greater facility than anyone else.'

I could not argue with his deductions and tackled him concerning the other two brothers.

'How about Brother Chef?'

'I have noticed that he relies a good deal upon the advice of others. He is a good plain cook but could not hold down a job in a restaurant. Brother Pisces, for example, had to help him with the cleaning and stuffing of the carp. I will look forward to learning more of him when I can do so without creating suspicion. The same I must say concerning Brother Reaper who I have noticed is often also referred to as Brother Orchard. These two brothers are worthy of further observation.'

CHAPTER 4

The Terror Strikes Again

At the next opportunity Holmes and I were determined to learn more about Brother Chef and Brother Reaper. I volunteered to assist Brother Chef in the preparation and cooking of a rabbit pie. I confess that I did not enjoy skinning the rabbits whilst he made the pastry, but at least I had a chance to converse with him in a manner which could hardly be suspect.

'You seem to be making a good job of that pastry, Brother. I imagine you have been long experienced in the kitchen?'

He was open in his reply. 'I had little experience in the kitchen when I came here, Brother Healer, but Prior Culthorpe only had an opening for a chef when making up his Secret Seven. My experience did not really lie in that direction, having spent some years as a chemist, working in a laboratory where experiments were carried out upon animals. I was never very happy with these experiments, however beneficial they may have been for mankind, so when I learned about the Secret Seven I wanted to become one of them in order to meditate for a while. I may not spend the rest of my life here, but I have the opportunity to decide upon my future. The irony of the situation, Brother, is that I have been able to stop the deliberate infliction of diseases in animals in favour of wringing the necks of chickens and dissecting fish and rabbits!'

That he had a sense of humour I could tell and I was forced to laugh at his grisly joke. But my ears had pricked up a little at his mention of his work in the laboratory. A knowledge of poisons was, after all, something which interested us in finding a suspect.

When later I told Holmes of what I had learned concerning Brother Chef he whistled, rather with amusement than in surprise.

'Upon my word, Watson, to have a man who is skilled in the use of poisons as a chef is indeed ironic. Of course, were he the culprit for whom we seek it would surprise me in that he was so open in the admission to you of his background. But we cannot rule him out, for stranger things have happened.'

I enquired, 'Did you learn anything from Brother Reaper as you planned to do?'

'I spent a pleasant hour with him; seeking him out in his orchard. His knowledge of the propagation of fruit trees appears to be considerable. Moreover, he has more to do than most, being for the moment Brother Reaper as well. My work with the bees is minimal by comparison. This fact enabled me to offer my help in the pruning of his bushes. He became quite loquacious and indeed I will spare you the greater part of his narrative, but he evidently ran his own cider-bottling business at one time. However, he lost his well-established orchard and thus his strain of cider apples which had been in his family for generations.'

'Do you mean that he lost it in the financial sense?'

'As it happens, no, he lost it through a particularly virulent strain of blight which attacked his trees. I try to open my mind to most useful knowledge as you know, but I confess I know little concerning fruit trees. From what he told me it would seem to have been something like that scourge of the elm trees in Holland, where a pestilent beetle attacks the bark. However, the Dutch have combated this by the encouragement of a certain small bird of the chaffinch family which rids the elm of its tormentors if given the opportunity. Brother Orchard tried to find an avian variety to do the same for his fruit trees, but in introducing a flock of starlings he found that he lost his fruit to them. In any case his efforts were too little and too late. So when he heard that Culthorpe needed a Brother Orchard he felt that he had little to lose in volunteering for the post.'

'What do you make of him as a suspect, Holmes?'

My friend did not immediately reply, but when he did it was clear that he had given the matter considerable thought.

'I do not discount him entirely, Watson, but I can see no motive based upon my present knowledge. It would be a little far fetched to surmise that he has recreated his superb cider apple since working on Culthorpe's orchard would it not?'

I replied, 'Extremely, given the short time involved, and the other circumstances.'

He rounded on me sharply. 'What other circumstances?'

I realized that I had been speaking my idle thoughts aloud and tried to justify my words.

'Well, if he were to destroy Culthorpe and the rest of us, it would scarcely present him with the ownership of the orchard.'

'Exactly, but you have brought out into the light a point which we have not until now considered, or at least discussed.'

'And that is?'

'That we are ourselves in just as much danger as the rest of the brethren. We must be alert at all times, Watson: we are here to save lives, and two of them may be our own. Oh, by the way, Brother Orchard mentioned one other interesting fact which although of no direct connection with our investigations may beguile the historian in you. It would appear that a battle occurred upon these very meadows and around this particular building during the troubles between Cornwall's Puritans and the Royalist Cavaliers!'

I was surprised that Culthorpe had not mentioned this during our long conversations concerning Grimstone Priory. I said as much but Holmes did not seem to consider this important.

'My dear Watson, the man has rather a lot upon his mind and could most easily decide to forego an account of a skirmish between Cavaliers and Roundheads, however fascinating.'

None the less he could see no harm in my bringing up the subject at the meal table. So that is what I did with surprisingly dramatic effect.

Culthorpe said, 'I did not mention it to you, Brother

Healer, because as a man of science you would have dismissed any account of supernatural manifestations. You see, through the years, at quite wide intervals there have been accounts of a phantom army of Royalists quite suddenly appearing at midnight in the three-acre meadow: that is the one directly before the front of the house. An old retainer of mine claimed to have seen and heard them some years ago. He was scared almost out of his wits and left at the break of day never to return.'

He turned to Holmes. 'What do you make of this, Brother Hive?'

Holmes said, 'An interesting account of the ravings of a senile mind.'

'But he had shown no previous sign of senility; besides which there have been other, similar accounts of such manifestations: from even more reliable quarters.'

At this point the subject was changed and I felt that Culthorpe did not wish to delve too deeply into the subject; perhaps in a desire not to alarm any of the brethren.

Holmes and I strolled in the grounds, ostensibly to enjoy a pipe in the garden. My friend was a little dismissive of the talk of a 250-year-old civil war and any connection it might have with our interests.

'By the way, Watson, I will be making an expedition to Hurstpierpoint on the morrow, so I know I can rely upon you to keep an eagle eye upon everything here.'

I wondered at what the nature of such an expedition might take but he spared me having to enquire when he volunteered . . .

'I will be going to the local library and reading-rooms

where doubtless there will be a collection of local newspapers covering the past half-century. I am anxious to see if I can turn up anything of interest concerning Grimstone Priory. I would be grateful, however, if you would keep the nature of my errand to yourself. I would rather even Culthorpe should be kept unaware of my activities. I will leave the house following breakfast to tend my hives and I will rely upon you to try and draw attention away from my absence should I be missed. I will take bread and cheese with me as if intending to spend a day in the fields.'

Holmes was as good as his word, setting off immediately after breakfast upon the day which followed, with provender wrapped in a kerchief, occasioning no raised eyebrow. I was anxious to observe everything around me but for the very first time it fell out that my services as a healer were required. Brother Pisces had caught his thumb in a fish hook and I was required to cleanse the wound which was a little bit more serious than might be supposed. Then there was Culthorpe himself with sprained wrist which proved to need no more than a little strapping. I felt that he had made much of a very slight injury in order to be able to speak with me in private. He not unnaturally enquired regarding Holmes's progress. I told him that my friend would himself prefer to give him a report upon our findings. Then realizing that I might have risked the confidentiality required I followed up quickly with a suggestion that such a report should be on the day following. This appeared to satisfy him and I breathed more easily.

My next task was to help Brother Chef in the kitchen where I took on the task of cleaning and stuffing a fish. It was again a carp, but a smaller one than I had seen before; though large by normal standards. As I cleaned it I discovered a small hard pear-like object inside it. Indeed at first I thought it was in fact a pearl but Brother Chef pooh-pooh-ed this, saying, 'Only oysters and some other shellfish produce pearls. It is probably an ossified fish egg, part of the ovum the rest of which the fish has expelled.'

Then he appeared to lose interest in it and I dropped the object into the pocket of my habit. I had stuffing to make from the breadcrumbs, sage, thyme and onion slices; I mixed it with milk and water and forced it into the cavity that my cleaning activities had produced in the fish. Then with needle and thread I sewed up the fish, like a surgeon repairing the cuts made by his scalpel. It was an interesting skill that I was learning, one which I mused might stand me in good stead should I ever be marooned upon a desert island like Robinson Crusoe in the classic tale.

When Brother Orchard threatened to take some fruit to the hives for my friend I hastily volunteered to take it. I did in fact take the bag of pears to the hives where, to my amazement, I perceived the figure of Sherlock Holmes even from a fair distance. I would not have been able to recognize his features from so far but could make out distinctly a figure in an apiarist's protective headpiece and could hardly have assumed it to be anyone else. However, when I reached the hives I discovered that the headpiece and mesh gown had been arranged upon staves to give the impression of a person tending the bees. I never cease to marvel at Sherlock Holmes's ingenuity!

The afternoon I spent with Brother Shepherd who showed

me how to pare the hooves of a sheep. (Another useful trade if I am ever made to follow in Selkirk's footsteps.) As ever, he spoke openly and politely, and I told him the tale about Brother Hive expecting a swarm. When I asked his opinion regarding the story of the phantom Royalists he replied, 'I cannot discount the story, Brother Healer, for I have seen so many strange things in my time; though I could explain most of them away if I chose to. Sometimes, however, I do *not* choose to!'

I thought this a very sage remark.

The rest of the day I spent trying to look busy and at the same time keeping a wary eye that nobody made for the hives.

When Holmes arrived back he eased his way in by making for the hives first. In this way he was able to be seen to be walking from their direction, towards the house, as if he had been all day with the bees. I had little to tell him but looked forward to hearing if his expedition to the library had been fruitful. Even if it had I had no idea what to expect from it and had to wait until the other brothers had retired before Holmes told me of his enquiries. As we sat by the dying glow of one of the last fires perhaps until autumn, be told me of his findings.

'I must speak softly, Watson, lest we should be over-heard, though I have no reason to believe that we might be. I found the library to be quite impressive in its scope, for aside from the usual section for its members to borrow books of fiction and general interest I noted that its reference section was all that I had hoped for. I found some reference works upon Grimstone Priory just as I had hoped to, and learned that Culthorpe's version of its history was accurate enough; also I did find reference to the battle between Royalist and Commonwealth armies of which we have been but recently informed. Evidently the supporters of King Charles were defeated and as they made retreat they vowed to return.'

I asked, 'Did you find anything of more recent interest?'

He paused as if preparing for a fairly long narration, which indeed was to follow.

'It was not until I got to a study of the files of the *Hurstpierpoint Argus* that I found anything worthy of notation. I will read to you the page from my notebook which I filled by copying a news item concerning a robbery . . .

THEFT AT GRIMSTONE PRIORY

This morning we learned from the Secretary to Lord Grimstone that his Lordship had suffered a tragic theft of family jewels and heirlooms which had been stored in a room in one of the towers at his ancestral home, Grimstone Priory. Only Lord Grimstone had a key to the tower. The jewels had seemingly vanished without trace when His Lordship visited the tower on one of his regular tours of inspection. There seemed no way that the items could have been carried out of the building unobserved. The unglazed window slots were too small for anything of a size larger than a man's fist to pass through, and in any case objects passed through could only fall into the moat, some thirty feet below. It is understood that the jewels were for the most part very large unmounted stones, which had been collected by the Grimstone family through the ages with the ultimate plan of using them to be mounted in coronets and amulets and such formal wear. This now may never happen unless the stolen items are recovered. The present

Lord Grimstone is the last of his line and has informed *The Argus* (through his Secretary) that he would not care to start a new collection. We understand that the stones were somewhat under-insured with Lloyd's.

'So the plot thickens does it not, Watson? I cannot see that the stolen jewels of Lord Grimstone have much to connect them to Culthorpe and his threatened secret order; yet one cannot refuse to collect any data connected with this Priory. I spoke with the librarian at length, telling him that I was staying at this place with the intention of writing a learned work upon its history. He volunteered much interesting yet probably irrelevant information. For instance, that Lord Grimstone paid many of his debts with the insurance money but still managed to be heavily in debt a few years later when he died suddenly. The Priory was then sold to Culthorpe at what is known as a knockdown price.'

I said, 'Lloyd's must have been happy enough that the jewels were unlikely to be regained, for they are as insurers beyond reproach and yet extremely thorough on behalf of their shareholders.'

'Quite so, Watson, and I am sure that we would be wasting our time should we visit the tower in question. Yet I cannot resist doing just that. Would you care to join me upon an illicit search of the tower?'

'Would it not be better to wait until the morrow and gain permission of Culthorpe? Especially as we do not know which tower is the one in question.'

Holmes glared at me. 'Oh come, my dear fellow, where is

your sense of adventure? Oh, and the librarian indicated that it was the tower that is upon one's left when entering the Priory!'

He rose, obviously determined to embark upon an illicit escapade which I could hardly refuse to join in with him.

'I believe this is the spiral staircase that we need to climb.'

With some trepidation I followed him.

We mounted that winding staircase as quietly as our wooden sabots would allow. Then at the top, I for my part somewhat breathless but Holmes not at all affected by the climb, we came upon a heavy oaken door with a large antique example of the locksmith's art. The incorrigible Sherlock Holmes made short work of opening it with his pocket knife. He used the blade normally reserved for removing stones from the hooves of horses. This is not to suggest that the lock was primitive despite its age; rather does it suggest that Sherlock Holmes is a housebreaker *par excellence*.

'We should have brought some oil for those hinges, Watson.'

Holmes referred to the creaking of the hinges which I hoped would not attract attention by awakening sleeping brethren. There is not much to see, Holmes.'

I was disappointed at the sight of the empty, all but circular, apartment. Holmes, however, seemed quite intrigued.

'Watson, let us imagine that we were intent upon stealing Grimstone's family jewel collection. We have established that we could have fairly easily gained entry to this tower. What would our next move be?'

'To transport the precious stones from this place to somewhere outside the Priory.'

'Quite so, now how would we do that? In those days there were doubtless guards and servants to contend with.'

'We could drop the booty out of the window onto the grass below.'

'According to the librarian there was a moat, deep with fetid water and thick with weeds. The grass was put there by Culthorpe when he filled the moat.'

I took his point that the felon would find it nigh impossible to recover anything dropped into such a trough of stinking water. We were about to examine the floor for some overlooked trifle that might furnish Holmes with more information when we were startled by a cry from below. I thought at first that our midnight escapade had been discovered, but Holmes insisted that the cries came from the grounds without.

Hastily we retreated from the tower, locking it behind us and quietly descending the stairs. At ground level we quickly placed ourselves in the entrance hall to which we would have naturally migrated upon hearing the cries.

'Brother Hive, Brother Healer, did you hear a blood-curdling cry?'

We answered Culthorpe in the affirmative; then Holmes was on his way to the grounds in the front of the Priory. We followed, having difficulty in matching his pace.

'Look . . . look to the left and to the right of you!'

We did as Holmes bade us and saw to our astonishment what appeared to be a group of horsemen in each of the two directions. Those to the right appeared to be wearing large brimmed hats from which blew ostrich feathers. The riders to the left seemed to be clad in steel helmets. Both groups had a ghostly glow which indeed made the blood run cold. But the riders sat on their horses and made no movement, neither did they utter a sound, for the cries had emanated and were still emanating from Brother Shepherd who stood upon the drive, equidistant to both equine groups.

'Dear Lord, what on earth does this mean?'

Culthorpe breathed his astonishment; yet there was no fear in his voice. Then suddenly the horses on both sides of us reared up, then wheeled and were gone within seconds. But more than seconds elapsed before any of us spoke.

Brother Shepherd quivered with anxiety as he turned to us.

'Did you see what I saw? Two groups of horsemen from the time of the civil war, an eerie glow to each of them; I tell you they were unearthly, not of this world. It is some sort of sign, and perhaps we should leave this place . . .'

We left Culthorpe to soothe Brother Shepherd, Holmes whispering to me to investigate the ground to the left. He ran in pursuit of the hoof marks of the Cavaliers' horses. We both examined the ground where the horsemen had been. I for one being overjoyed to find hoof prints, suggesting that the riders had been of the earthly flesh-and-blood variety. Within a minute or two we had both rejoined Culthorpe and Shepherd, the latter now much calmer.

'What do you make of it, Brother Hive?'

Culthorpe showed his composure by not forgetting to address Holmes thus. My friend replied, 'On my side a dozen flesh-and-blood horses ridden by appropriately clad riders, their costumes treated with phosphorous. How about your findings, Brother Healer?'

I said, 'I find honest-to-goodness hoof prints and traces of phosphorous on the shrubs against which they had brushed.'

Brother Shepherd said, 'I realize now that this is yet another attempt to make the Secret Seven no more. Yet this time there seemed to be no actual danger to anyone involved.'

Holmes said, 'Brother Shepherd, we do not even know that there is a connection. There may be a logical answer to the riddle presented to us tonight.'

We had hoped that the other brothers might not have seen the phantom riders but at breakfast it soon proved to be otherwise. All had espied the strange opposing groups from the windows through which they had peered when Brother Shepherd had cried out.

Later, when the chance occurred for us to openly discuss what had happened, Holmes remarked to me, 'There are several intriguing points to emerge from this business of the ghostly armies, Watson. First, if it is a hoax aimed at scaring off the Secret Seven the stakes must be high, because the hire of two dozen horses with riders and period costumes could not be an inexpensive enterprise. Second, I find it far from easy to believe that the subject of conversation bringing in the battle and the ghostly armies previously seen could hardly have been coincidental in its introduction just hours before this incident.'

I grasped the two points that he had made. Whoever had staged the ghostly riders had made sure that their past legend was remembered. Also this staging could not have been cheap. Where would our tormentor recruit these equestrian thespians? If he also needed to buy their silence as well as their dramatics. Then another question, delayed through recent dramatic events, returned to my mind.

'Holmes, do you think there could be a connection between these mysteries that surround the Secret Seven and the theft of the Grimstone jewels?'

'I wondered when you would ask me that question, Watson. The answer is that I do feel that there is a possibility of a connection. But if not there is certainly some other very valuable motive involved.'

'Yet we are discussing a crime which has already taken place; the jewels were stolen some years ago.'

My friend smiled enigmatically. 'I think if I could answer all your questions at this moment in time it would make our task very easy and yet would take all the interest and pleasure from our work. The answer to that question may take a little more time and deduction. I fear it is a little more than a three-pipe problem. In fact, Watson, we may have to part company for a day or so, for I fear I may have to return to Baker Street; yet I dare not leave this place unguarded so will rely upon you to keep your eyes and ears wide open.'

CHAPTER 5

Brother Healer Holds the Fort

My friend's departure back to the relative peace and safety of Baker Street was not quite as simply accomplished as all that. He needed to go, I understood it, but he would have to step out of character in order to do it. We discussed all possibilities; wires from sick relatives, his expulsion by Prior Culthorpe, or even a staged arrest. Anything which would not reveal his real identity or his real occupation at Grimstone Priory. In the end, after discussion with Culthorpe, we decided that Holmes, in his guise as Brother Hive, should announce that he had changed his mind about life as a member of the Secret Seven. The others could make of this what they wished, but after the events of the past twelve hours it seemed logical and believable.

'Brethren, I have a painful but rather important announcement to make.'

Culthorpe gained the attention of us all and then continued, 'Brother Hive has decided to leave us: evidently life as a brother member of the Secret Seven does not entirely appeal to him after all. I feel sure that recent events have nothing to do with his decision, and I release him to resume life in the cruel outside world. You have my blessing, Brother; none of us wish you anything but well.'

There were grunts around the table; some of genuine concern for the brother who had proved unequal to his task, others with a tinge of irony.

Brother Shepherd asked, 'May one enquire if there is to be another Brother Hive soon, for the bees will need to be tended as usual.'

Culthorpe answered, 'I will renew my search for an experienced apiarist. Meanwhile, perhaps Brother Healer would take on his friend's work, on a purely temporary basis of course.'

I could only nod dumbly and wonder how I would manage the bees, which I neither understood nor found particularly interesting. I was caught in a trap.

Brother Pisces grumbled, 'Well, I hope whoever we get will be able to produce a decent jar of honey.'

Brother Orchard said, 'Come, let us not judge our brother; may he find peace somewhere else. He has a talent with the bees, but evidently he has not the nerve to stand up to the tribulations he finds here at the moment. That is not his fault.'

Sherlock Holmes, in his role as Brother Hive, should at this point have been given an award for his brilliant theatrical performance. He rose unsteadily and spoke in a voice that shook with nervousness.

'Brothers, I have failed you and I am full of anguish. I joined this brotherhood for the peace which I was assured it would bring me. Instead I found threats and manifestations which appeared to me to be of a supernatural nature. I must return to the comparative calm of the city.'

Culthorpe took Holmes to the station in his dogcart and I accompanied them; ostensibly to see my friend safely on his way but in fact so that the three of us could discuss matters pertinent and private.

'When will you be in contact with Dr Watson and myself?'

'My dear Culthorpe, I cannot answer that question at this moment in time but it will be in a matter of days rather than weeks. Watson will, of course, represent my interests here during my absence and I trust you will both continue to keep his and my true identity a secret. It pained to leave under a cloud, but I will redeem my good name with the brethren when I have brought this enigma to a satisfactory conclusion.'

I was a little worried on one score, 'How shall I contact you, Holmes? At Baker Street?'

'Why yes, for if I am elsewhere a message care of Mrs Hudson will find me. But I have every confidence in bringing this matter to a grand finale in a short while.'

As my friend climbed onto the train I shook his hand and wished him the very best of luck with his investigations, assuring him of my best efforts on his behalf.

The most unfortunate consequence of Holmes's departure, at least for myself, was that I got very badly stung by a swarm of bees and had to administer my healing powers to myself by applying a blue bag. Brother Orchard offered to help with the apiary and I was glad to leave it mainly in his capable hands.

'You need a special touch with bees, Brother, which you do not unfortunately have. Your friend now, he was a different matter. What a pity he is of such a timid character.'

I would like to be able to tell the reader at this point that the next day or two were without any serious incident. However, this I cannot in all conscience do. On the day that followed Holmes's departure a terrifying incident occurred. Brother Shepherd burst back into the priory immediately following breakfast, which he had left to tend his flock. He was distraught.

'Brothers, someone has killed all of my new season's lambs!'

Culthorpe was the first to reply. 'Do you mean, Brother Shepherd, that your lambs have been killed by some predator, perhaps a fox?'

'No, Brother Prior. They have had their throats slit, with a knife. It is dreadful, there is blood everywhere.'

I said, 'If the lambs are lying where they were killed, as I assume is so, they must have been destroyed from sheer bestial violence rather than for any plan for gain. A poacher or gypsy would have taken the bodies away to sell.'

'Come and see for yourselves, brethren, if you can bear to look upon such carnage.'

It was a gruesome sight with the innocent lambs lying inert and bloodstained. The ewes stood around them with a look of blank innocent bewilderment. It was terrible: a town dweller like myself does not really enjoy the thought of lambs being slaughtered even for commerce. I examined the knife, evidently the implement of destruction which lay beside one of the lamb carcasses, still red with gore. I held it up to the light and declared, 'It is a fruit-paring knife; have any of you seen it before?'

Brother Orchard said, 'I have one just like it, though I cannot be sure that it is mine until I have seen if it is missing.'

He rushed to his storage shed and returned almost at once.

'Brother Healer, mine is missing from its place upon the shelf, so I can only assume that it is mine.'

Although the fact that Orchard's knife had been used did not suggest that he was the culprit one had to bear its ownership in mind. Sadly we set about the task of burying the lambs, for we were agreed that none of us would have been able to eat lamb or mutton for a very long time.

Sadly and with heavy hearts we went through the motions of performing our tasks, and at meals there was a strange air of quietness that one could not associate with meditation.

When alone with Culthorpe I said, 'I am afraid I must suggest that this grisly incident is a further work of he, or she, who wishes ill to your association of seven. If Holmes were here I am certain that he would say the same thing.'

Drily he said, 'It is most unfortunate that he whom I have hired to investigate the whole matter has chosen to be absent, just when his presence might have been helpful.'

I defended my friend. 'On the surface what you say may seem valid; yet he may well be investigating that which controls such bestiality. I think we agreed earlier that we are dealing with a foe who is not only ruthless but has considerable resources.'

He grunted. 'But perhaps the knife might have told him more than you were able to learn from it.'

I was forced to admit that this could have been so. I could only hope that no further bizarre happening would occur during Holmes's absence, or at all for that matter. I penned a letter to Holmes informing him of what had happened in the hope that what information I could give would be useful, but more, that he might decide to return.

By return I received a letter, addressed to me in Holmes's hand, but it had a Norfolk postmark. This told me that he probably would not have as yet received my own letter. None the less I was anxious to read what he had to tell me. To my surprise the letter was a very long one, written closely on several foolscap sheets.

HOLMES'S LETTER.

Norwich April 16th.

My Dear Watson,

I know that you will be managing things without me in your usual quietly confident manner.

After I reached Baker Street I allowed myself an hour or two to enjoy the wonders of civilization. Then it was to work and I did quite some study upon the matter of the civil war between the Commonwealth and the forces of King Charles. When I learned that there are a number of organizations who keep the memory of those battles alive I became intrigued. I contacted the nearest person connected to them and whose name and address I was able to find. He turned out to be one Sir Arthur Carrington who resided upon his estate in Surrey where he staged mock battles between employees of his and the local villagers. (His own small private army being not unnaturally the Cavaliers!) I went to see him and it was quite an experience, Watson, for the man tries to live still as if he were the staunch right hand of Charles the First. He still cannot reconcile himself to the eventual victory by the Commonwealth powers and spends his life in trying to work out just where the king's men went wrong; re-staging the battles so that Charles's defeats can be rectified. In his study, which is lined with books and framed maps of the battlefields, he has a huge table which is set out with what you and I would refer to as tin soldiers with which he appears to practise his battle tactics. I gave him some idea of the information I was seeking and he in his turn put me in touch with a showman who hires out uniformed and costumed horsemen to whoever will pay.

This person, who calls himself Sir Richard Forrest, owns a circus and operates his horse and rider hire business from his winter quarters near Ascot. Another journey and I was able to learn from this knight of the circus that he had in fact hired Roundheads and Cavaliers, a dozen of each, to a man who he said was obviously working as an agent for another. It was arranged that the two groups of riders, daubed in luminous costumes, were to gather at each side of Grimstone Priory at midnight. The drill was that they were to ride toward each other and then halt. There was to be no uttered sound, simply gestures and then, as soon as they had been seen by a few persons they were to wave, then wheel about and silently ride off; the two groups in opposite directions. Forrest considered it a strange request, but as the pay was good he was happy to oblige in staging the event. He said, 'I could see no harm in it save perhaps for the minor fact of trespass, which at worst might land me with a five-pound fine.' Then he took me to see a group of huge and fearsome-looking lions, suggesting that I might wish to hire them!

So you see, Watson, we know now where our ghost riders

emanated from, although we have as yet no names of the perpetrators. Forrest insisted that no names were given and there was no written contract. He said: 'A handshake was good enough for me, having seen the colour of his money, but as you are Sherlock Holmes I will tell you that this go-between was a little fellow, rather seedy looking, who said that the purpose was a harmless practical joke to be played upon some people at this Priory.'

Well, Watson, that is my news, just to show you that I have not been idle and will of course be following my trails. But as to your own information: my dear fellow, what a dreadful scene must have been that slaughter of the lambs! I only wish I could have been there to support you, but I must complete my present investigations. I know that I can trust you to keep alert and to try and prevent any other bizarre events. Our foe – or is it foes – seems mercifully to have given up for the moment upon his seeming original plan of eliminating the Secret Seven one by one, perhaps having realized that he may gain his ends by less drastic means.

I trust you are tending the bees as well as you can. On this subject please avoid the shed which is in the copse a short way from the hives. I mention this because if you were to open the door you might disturb a latent swarm which I have in there. Warn others to avoid it too.

Please continue to keep me informed: I rely so much upon your help.

I remain, Your Sincere Friend,

Sherlock Holmes.

I put down the letter with mixed feelings: pleased that my friend continued to have such trust in me, yet quietly annoyed that he considered it more important to go about seeking the sources of ghostly riders rather than to be present to investigate a truly dreadful turn of events. However, then I considered the fact that Sherlock Holmes could not reveal his real identity to the brothers, and as far as returning as Brother Hive he had rather burnt his boats.

When I next came upon Brother Orchard I warned him about the shed in the copse. Not mentioning Holmes's letter I allowed him to believe that Brother Hive had warned me about the latent swarm before his departure. No one but Orchard was likely to visit that area so I thought that it would not be necessary to mention it elsewhere. As it was, Brother Orchard was puzzled, saying that he had never heard of a latent swarm, but he simply shrugged as if it were my own business only now.

I exercised extreme vigilance during the day, aye and the night which followed, feeling that even if Sherlock Holmes did not choose himself to exercise such alert vigilance I would not be found wanting. So I watched by night, from my window and on periodic traverses of the grounds, making up for my lack of sleep with the odd cat nap by day. I kept my nocturnal activity to myself, therefore the brethren inclined to think that I was rather lazy by day. But I decided to keep up this regime if there was any possibility that through its use I could prevent another bestial attack upon innocent livestock.

This procedure revealed nothing unusual until upon the third night I caught sight of a small human figure outlined against the skyline near the hives. The figure was small enough to be a boy of perhaps twelve or thirteen years. I at once took myself up to the area of the hives and found footprints made by hobnailed boots of a small size which seemed to have taken their wearer into the copse. They led directly to the shed and I felt sorry for the youngster if he had intruded upon the latent swarm. Yet by the light of my lamp I could see that the padlock was undisturbed, so the fact that the shed was locked had perhaps daunted him.

I mentioned the incident to Culthorpe the next day when a suitable moment presented itself. He said, 'No doubt it was a village boy, up to mischief. They hang around here at night sometimes, but have so far proved to be quite harmless. I imagine the shed had merely excited his curiosity.'

But alas that which was not quite so harmless was discovered. When Brother Pisces whose turn it was to tend the hens went to the chicken house he found that the poor creatures had been decapitated with an axe, which implement, like the knife in the slaughter of the lambs, had been left at the scene. It was with a heavy heart that I wrote this news to Holmes.

My Dear Holmes,

I thank you for your recent letter explaining your discoveries regarding the ghostly riders. But useful as this may be to the investigation as a whole I really do feel that your presence here would be of more value at the moment. There has been another ghastly incident, almost as gruesome as the slaughter of the lambs. Eight hens have been discovered beheaded. The axe, evidently the one used (for it is bloodstained) had been left carelessly in the chicken house. I managed (despite my lack of scientific equipment) to establish that the blood was indeed that of the hens (or certainly chicken blood at least). Very little noise would appear to have been made for I would have heard it had there been a commotion. This leads me to believe, Holmes, that the killer was someone to whom the poultry had become accustomed. They are foolish birds and would probably stand about watching one of their number being beheaded. (Quite a different matter with the lambs I imagine; but then that particular slaughter would have been performed at a distance and at a time when no night vigil was being kept.)

After this incident I will have to redouble my vigilance, especially at night; although the strain of the lack of sleep is making this difficult. I may feign illness and try to catch some sleep during the day. Fortunately there has been little call upon me as healer of late; also there seems little that I can do for the bees which seem almost to be looking after themselves.

I beg you to consider carefully my words concerning the need for your presence.

I remain, your friend,
Sincerely,

John H. Watson.

Whilst in the village posting my letter to Holmes I reflected that I might have overstepped the mark in all but criticizing my friend's actions and absence from the Priory. But I posted it after much soul searching. Then I took the long way back to the Priory in the hope that I might be able to use that time in constructive thought. I considered everything that had happened since Holmes had undertaken to try to solve the mystery of the Secret Seven. To begin with, two of the seven brethren had died of cyanide poisoning, which Holmes had eventually discovered. The vendetta had continued and our sharp wariness concerning further attempts in the direction had proved unneeded, for our antagonist appeared to have changed his tactics to those of terrifying the survivors rather than murdering them; as was evident from the incident of the ghostly riders and the slaughter of innocent farm stock. I wondered if this had been the plan all along; the shock of the two deaths and the eventual driving away of the rest of the brothers through a campaign of terror. But who could say with such a ruthless foe that he might not return to his murderous ways if the less drastic steps did not work for him. To add to the mystery there was the issue of the missing jewels from the tower which Holmes had decided had been flung through the window aperture and into a moat which had since been filled in. Holmes had insisted that the recovery of those jewels from the moat must at the time have been near to impossible. The thief must have known this, and yet had performed the reckless act. Of course I had to consider it more than likely that the theft and the threats against the monks were entirely unconnected!

As I walked, confident in being entirely on my own I spoke my thoughts aloud, mostly in the form of questions addressed to Sherlock Holmes. I often did this when alone and when having a problem to solve. I would ask my absent friend a question and then try to imagine what his reply would be. Unfortunately his answers, those that I had conjured up in my mind, had been of no great help to me in this instance, so I arrived back at Grimstone Priory older but by no means wiser.

During the next two days the brethren appeared calm yet watchful. They tended the surviving livestock constantly as if fearing that the butchery might be repeated. Eventually another letter arrived for me from Sherlock Holmes, but it was not particularly reassuring.

My Dear Watson,

My grateful thanks for your latest report. I am so sorry that you have needed to face up to another horrific incident without my support but I can assure you that you are serving my needs splendidly, however helpless you may feel. If it were not vital for me to be away from the Priory I can promise you that I would not be taking the course that I follow.

Please try to reassure Culthorpe as to the purpose of my activities and tell him that I have every expectation of bringing the case to a satisfactory conclusion in a matter of days.

No doubt you are yourself just as anxious to hear about my present activities. Well, all will be made clear to him and to your good self in a very short while. Meanwhile I have found the perfect replacement for myself at the Priory: a Mr Izaak Tapforth who is a real apiarist, in need of temporary peaceful seclusion and a period in which to reflect. No need, by the way, for Culforth to tell the brothers that he is only a locum, so to speak. Explain that he is a nervous man, fond of keeping his own council and whilst trustworthy in every way is not at all sociable.

Tapforth should be arriving within a few hours of this letter. Do not press him to converse for reasons that I have given.

Meanwhile please bear with your Sincere friend,

Sherlock Holmes.

As I returned the letter to its envelope I noted that it was written with a pencil, so I assumed that Holmes had not written it at Baker Street although the postmark would suggest otherwise. He had given me no idea, despite his reassurances, as to his present activities. But Sherlock Holmes was a law unto himself and I had no reason to doubt that he was correct in his suggestion that he was on the brink of bringing the mystery of the Secret Seven to a satisfactory conclusion.

CHAPTER 6

The New Brother Hive

I replied to Holmes's letter, although I had little more to add and could hardly make much comment upon the impending arrival of Izaak Tapforth as this was a *fait accompli*. But whilst searching my pockets for my stamp case I came upon the pear-like stone, and remembered that I had meant to show it to Holmes. So I enclosed it in my letter with details of its acquisition. I did this more through having so little to report than through any feeling that the object could be of interest to him.

Evidently Holmes had sent word to Culthorpe about the impending arrival of Tapforth, for his appearance at the Priory occasioned no great surprise. He proved to be a tall man, with an extremely luxuriant beard and shoulder-length hair of a reddish-brown colour. He merely grunted his reply when I greeted him and shook hands with an extreme reluctance. He hurried to his cell and when he reappeared in friar's garb he had the hood raised even when he was inside the Priory. A very strange fellow, but mild and polite enough. Culthorpe introduced him to the brethren who greeted him with great reserve; rather as if expecting that he might take to his heels at the first sign of trouble.

It was my duty to take Tapforth to the hives to show him everything, but he seemed reluctant to even touch the slides or any other apiary equipment. After a few minutes I left him to it. However, when next I went to the apiary I found that all was well with every sign that he had put to rights the neglect of the past few days. I could only conclude that he was the type of man who did not like to be watched whilst performing his duties. Had I ever put my earlier thoughts into words I would have felt obliged to apologize to him for believing that he perhaps knew little about bees! For a couple of days a sort of uneasy calm descended upon Grimstone Priory, and I observed little to attract any sort of suspicion save another fleeting glimpse of the retreating form of that village boy as Culthorpe had suggested that he might be. This time I noticed that he carried a straw bag of the kind used by shoppers and sea anglers at the coast. But the incident did not worry me greatly following the last glimpse of him suggesting no particular phenomenon.

I would like to tell the reader that this period of tranquillity continued, but alas it proved to be the calm before the storm, or at least heavy weather. The night arrived when I was following one of my periodic tours of inspection when I heard a sound of a horse neighing, from the direction of the stable. Normally the horses were quiet at night, once they had been placed into their stalls, but at the same time I felt that a horse might decide to neigh for no reason more serious than a rat in its straw or a kicked-over water bucket. But then as I neared the stable I heard some kind of commotion from within and as I got nearer still I was surprised to see a male figure in the habit of the Secret Seven emerging, and the figure whisked past me, running at such speed that with my game leg I knew it would be useless for me to pursue him. To make things worse I was so startled that I could not recall any detail of him save that he wore a friar's habit with the hood raised over his head. I decided that my next move should be to ascertain if the horses were unhurt and safely in their stalls. This proved to be so, and just as I was feeling the fetlocks of one of them I heard a sound from a corner of the stable. It came from the area where the straw was piled and a smaller figure emerged from behind the straw and bolted for the door. This time I took up the chase and noted that he whom I pursued was the so-called village boy of previous fleeting glimpses, or if not another just like him.

But alas my chase of the small fleeting figure was useless and by the time I reached a clump of trees into which he had disappeared I knew that I had lost him. So I made my way back to the Priory which I entered and picked up the striker and banged the dinner gong with considerable force. This brought forth eventually the brothers, with Culthorpe the first to appear. I made sure that they were all present and cast an eye across them looking for any sign of a recent expedition out of doors, but could see none.

'Brother Healer, whatever is the matter?'

I answered Culthorpe's question. 'I heard a horse neigh, and as I neared the stables a brother in habit emerged and made off. In ascertaining that the horses were unharmed I surprised a lad, or very small man, who also eluded my pursuit.'

All of the brethren appeared to be horrified and in their turns expressed concern.

'The horses are safe?'

'We must inspect them now . . .'

'Who could have had business in the stable?'

I said, 'We will make our way there now that we may ensure the well-being of the horses, which at a cursory inspection appeared unhurt. The figure in the habit would scarcely have made off had one of our number been involved. I suspect another, in habit as disguise against possible sighting. As for the lad, he was doubtless an accomplice in some wrongdoing.'

We all of us went to the stables and found the horses well, if somewhat disturbed by recent events.

We calmed them and Culthorpe suggested, 'We must each take our turn at watching the stables by night. The lambs and fowl were a sad loss, and cruelly caused: but the horses are of even more importance. They are not only our faithful servants, but most of us number them among our dear friends.'

It was agreed that we would take turns at watching the horses by night. I was all for informing the police concerning this latest threat.

When we were alone I said to Culthorpe, 'Come, sir, we have too long neglected to ask the authorities for help.'

But he said, 'No, Doctor, we cannot bring in the police; it would draw public attention to the Secret Seven and destroy our seclusion. Did I not call upon your friend Holmes in order to avoid such a step? I am beginning to think that this was a mistake. I had the option of consulting Ferrers Locke, but felt that Sherlock Holmes was the best in the field. Perhaps, sir, in your accounts of his cases and exploits you have exaggerated his powers of deduction?'

I was furious because although I might have found reason to wonder at the recent activities of Sherlock Holmes I had no intention of allowing others to belittle him in my hearing.

Warmly I said, 'Far from exaggerating his powers I have if anything found it difficult to explain to my readers that all but psychic power which he seems at times to display in solving criminal cases.'

His lip curled a little. 'Really, then I hope that he will call upon the spirits very soon in aiding my predicament.'

I replied, perhaps a little too sharply, 'Your irony does not escape me, sir, and you well know that I referred to an almost uncanny power of deduction rather than to any supernatural power. He has written to tell me that he is close to a successful conclusion.'

Drily he said, 'I'm glad to hear it. He has written to me too, but only to tell me of this fellow Izaak Tapforth whom he has sent to look after my bees. He seems to be a rather strange fellow, rather withdrawn, or do you think he is perhaps a few pence short of a shilling?'

I said, 'I have checked on his work with the hives, and he seems to perform it well: perhaps more ably than did Holmes himself.'

His reply all but infuriated me. 'Well, well, perhaps we

can get him to solve our problems where Holmes seems to have fallen down as well?'

On the verge of losing my temper I yet calmed myself, saying, 'I believe you will be surprised by the events of the next few days, hours even!'

I hoped, oh how much I hoped that I was right. Could what was being said have a ring of truth. Had Holmes passed the best of his powers or was his seeming lack of concern a different aspect of some change of outlook? I tried to push such thoughts from my mind. Instead I tried to be subjective concerning the events of the night, using those methods made famous by the very man who seemed now to be doubted.

Perhaps the friar who had emerged from the stable had also heard the horse neigh and had gone to investigate. He had possibly not seen the intruder, hidden by the hay, yet suspected that there had been one. Perhaps also he had not been running away from me but believing that he saw some distant retreating figure. Meanwhile I had almost caught the village boy who was responsible for the whole incident. But why then had the brother concerned not admitted to what had happened? Perhaps he felt that the finger of suspicion would fall on him, as well it might have.

It is of course difficult for any balanced person to believe that anyone could kill or maim a creature as wonderful and faithful as a horse. But then one observes cruelty to horses almost daily upon the streets of London, mostly from cab drivers and those who hold the reins on drays and other delivery vehicles.

Then another train of thought occurred to me. Could it

have been that the village boy had surprised the friar in some ghastly deed and then hidden from me, thinking that suspicion might fall upon him? I felt sure that Holmes could have answered these questions to my satisfaction.

I sat down with a confused mind and heavy heart to write a report for Sherlock Holmes in which I presented him with all that had occurred and gave him a rather polite version of my conversation with Culthorpe. Two uneventful days later I received his reply:

My Dear Watson,

I am so grateful to you for being likely the saviour of the horses and I am glad that you have organized a guard system for them. However, as it is possible that the perpetrator is one of the brethren this would seem to have its problems. You will need to have two of the brothers at each watch.

As for Culthorpe; pray do not concern yourself with his criticism of my abilities for he will learn the truth very shortly, as will you too my good faithful friend.

Sincerely, as ever,

Sherlock Holmes.

I was heartened by his letter but none the less puzzled by his intentions. Quickly I organized the equine vigil with the aid of Culthorpe, who could at once see the point of two brothers being present at each watch.

He grunted and said, 'At least the fellow is doing something.'

The rest of that day I spent in fitful dozing in my cell,

anxious that I could be alert enough when night came to be active until dawn. Brother Orchard and I took the first watch which was completely uneventful and as he went yawning off to his bed and we were replaced by Brothers Pisces and Chef I pretended to be taking a brisk walk around the outside of the Priory before turning in. Instead, of course, I intended to keep a watch for the remainder of the night.

Feeling that it might be apt for once to watch the Priory from a distance rather than from close quarters I made for the copse which was near to the hives. On my way up there I cast an eye at the hives and noted the protective armour still supported upon staves where Holmes and I had left it. I was suddenly seized with a desire to examine the shed, deterred from this as I had been before with a fear of the rumoured inert swarm. I had no key to the padlock and lacked Holmes's nimble fingers in opening such things with penknives or pieces of wire. I peered through the little window but there was a sack hung inside it precluding any sort of a view.

At length, curiosity overcame my reticence and safe in the knowledge that all the brethren were either on watch or in their cots I decided to take the plunge so to speak. I felt that I might more easily unscrew the fittings for the padlock than pick the lock. I had a penknife which had several useful blades but all of them were pointed and not of very much use as a screwdriver. Indeed I tried to use the second largest blade in this way with disastrous results. First I cut myself, though not seriously, and then I broke the point of the blade in trying to use it for that purpose for which it was never designed. Then suddenly as I stared at the broken, no longer pointed, end I realized that I was looking at something which appeared very like a screw-driver. In breaking it I had modified it to fit my purpose!

It was still a formidable task to tackle the two strongly driven screws which prevented me from opening the door, but I realized that it was only a matter of time and effort. My energetic labours eventually enabled me to open the shed door.

'Upon my word!' I remember I gasped the words aloud as I shone my lamp around the interior of the shed. I could catch no sight of any inert swarm of bees, but I did see that a simple cot had been formed within, and there was a candle wedged into a bottle top, in addition there was a crate beside the cot upon which were the remains of a simple meal. The coffee pot was still warm and recent tobacco ash showed me that the shed had been in recent, very recent occupation. Some intruder, knowing of the whole situation at the Priory had taken up residence in a shed which he was doubtless aware that Holmes had for-bidden its examination.

Leaving the door swinging and not stopping even for the nicety of its closure I started down towards the Priory. Another half-minute and I would have been shouting for attention from those within. But as I passed the hives I received a terrifying shock as the protective suit and mask seemed to spring into uncanny activity, rearing up from where I had thought it to be simply supported by staves. But of course within seconds I realized that there could be nothing supernatural about this figure. I could barely make out human features through the mesh face-piece. I sprang into action, leaping at this advancing figure and grasping at the face-piece with the intention of removing it from the head of the intruder. But then as he laid his hands upon my shoulders and held me back I was amazed by the strength, aye and the length, of his arms. He spoke at last with a familiar incisive voice.

'My dear Watson, you have been of inestimable help to me so far; pray do not spoil it by awakening the brethren!'

He removed his face-piece and there stood Sherlock Holmes. As he removed the rest of the garment I noted that he was dressed in country tweeds and looked not at all as one would expect a man to look who had been dwelling in a shed.

'Holmes! How long have you been up here?'

'Almost from the start, Watson.'

'What do you mean by "the start"?'

'Oh I got off the train at the very next station and wired for Billy to bring me fresh clothing and other necessities.'

I gasped, 'So it was Billy who I mistook for an intruding village boy? But you answered my letters, the ones I sent to Baker Street!'

'Billy has been to and fro to London each day, and very helpful were your reports, my dear fellow.'

'It was a fiction then that you went to see this circus chap about the ghostly riders?'

'Only in that I went myself; I sent an agent of mine who reported to Billy.'

'Was it also Billy who I disturbed in the stable; and who then was the hooded figure who had emerged from there?'

'It was your humble servant, Watson. I had heard the disturbance before you did, and I surprised a hooded brother in the stable clearly up to no good. He got away from me, just as I got away from you later. After he eluded me, you see, I had returned to the stable to reassure myself concerning the horse. I naturally got some idea as to what the intruder might have been about following your reports concerning the slaughter of the other livestock. I was too late to prevent these atrocities, but in any case I needed to observe these happenings rather than reveal myself.'

'Then I cannot see what use my reports were; or what purpose you have served yourself.'

I spoke rather warmly, I regret to say. Holmes had used me in this manner before, notably in the case which I have published under the title of *The Hound of the Baskervilles*. This time, however, I was less furious than I had been on that occasion when Holmes had hidden out on the moors. I could see, after that experience, that my own ignorance of his presence was necessary.

So I simply muttered, 'You have made me feel like an idiot, sending you all that information of which you were already aware.'

'But you gave me valuable insights into events, feelings and reactions from inside the Priory, Watson. But forgive me, old friend, we cannot dally further because the game is afoot. I have reason to believe that another atrocity will take place tonight; or rather, this morning, for it is two of the clock. Who will be watching the horses at this moment in time?'

'Brothers Shepherd and Orchard.'

'Ah, quite so. Then the time has come for us to take ourselves to the fish pond.'

His words took me by surprise, but then so had the events of the past half-hour. I felt I could not do other than follow his directions and try to make myself of some use. Then, as we reached the pool; I saw what at first looked like piles of silver ornaments catching the moonlight. Instead, to my dismay, I realized that we were gazing at the piled-up bodies of a great many huge carp. We dropped to our knees to examine them; there were some forty to fifty of the huge fish; each and every one of them had been slit from below the gills to the vent. The fish had not been gutted, but merely slit, and of course killed. We looked around for a knife and we soon found one, bearing slime and scales. But more importantly we found a trawling net with traces of silvery scales upon it. The fish had been netted and not fished with rod and line.

As soon as I found it in me to speak I said, 'God, what a tragedy! Hundreds of years of carp husbandry ruined in a single night.'

To my surprise, Holmes was calm. 'Not at all, Watson! You will notice that all of the dead fish are of a very large size. This is not chance for if you examine the trawling net you will notice that the mesh is such that would allow lesser sized fish to escape. Whoever did this wanted only to dispatch the very largest of the carp. These I would estimate are aged between ten and fifty years. There are, you will observe, perhaps a hundred or so smaller fish still within the pool. Left undisturbed for a decade the situation will return to normal.'

'But Holmes, I do not understand! Why would someone

simply intent upon committing an atrocity be concerned with leaving the smaller fish? Surely their intention was to destroy and not to leave the possibility of rebirth of the carp?'

'We are dealing with a shrewd foe, Watson. He had no wish to destroy the carp pond or its future use; he was interested in these unfortunate fish alone.'

'Do you not consider the same bestial person performed this act and the slaughter of the lambs and chickens?'

'Oh indeed yes, Watson, but with one very great difference.'

'Which is?'

'The first two atrocities were pointless, save for a desire to draw attention. This present foul deed has been performed with a definite purpose in mind, which he hopes is masked by the pointless nature of the other slaughters.'

'So you mean that he wishes us to think that this is also pointless; but you feel that it is not?'

'Exactly so, Watson, exactly so. But I am afraid you must wait just a little longer for a complete explanation.'

'Which you could give me if you wished?'

'I could, Watson, but I have to thrust you back into the lions' den like Daniel of old. I do not wish you to betray that anyone is onto him.'

'He is present at the Priory then?'

'Indeed, but enough questions. You have to face breaking the news to your brother members of the Secret Seven.'

Holmes made his way silently back to the hives as with heavy heart I took myself into the Priory and struck the gong. Soon the brothers came, including the two from the stable. I explained what had happened and led them all to the pond where Brother Pisces flew into a most furious rage.

'What brute has done this, what unspeakable vandal has killed these beautiful carp, the largest and finest from my pond?'

Then he calmed himself and said, 'I beg your pardon, Brothers, I should have said *our* pond.'

Culthorpe, shaking with rage, said, 'Another pointless act of bestiality. Where will it end? Shepherd, Orchard, go to the stable and be sure that the horses are not attacked. We have not much else left unscathed.'

I tried to calm Brother Pisces, saying, 'There are plenty of small carp left, they will grow and multiply surely?'

He replied, 'Brother Healer, you were not here as I was, many years ago when the old lord had the carp removed from the moat and placed in the pond so that he could drain and plant that outdated defence. When I came back to tend the pond I found to my joy that it had not been touched since then, and those same fish had grown to huge proportions. Moreover, there were many smaller ones, proving their breeding ability and the ideal nature of their pond. I took them sparingly to feed us, knowing that with good husbandry there would be a rotation of big fish. Now my system is ruined . . . I don't want to see the pond again!'

He walked back towards the Priory, or rather dragged himself back there, with the gait of a broken man. I felt terribly concerned for him, and indeed for the other good brethren; I could not believe that one of their number was our adversary.

Culthorpe detained me as the others walked sadly away, saying, 'Watson, this latest outrage shows me what a terrible mistake I made in engaging Sherlock Holmes. During all this time he has not discovered my tormentor, nor yet been able to prevent his depravations. I fear that any contract that I entered into with him must be considered to be void.'

I rounded upon him. 'Culthorpe, you have no idea how much work my friend has entered into on your behalf. I admit it is unfortunate that he was unable to prevent the atrocities but this would have made his eventual discovery of the tormentor impossible.'

I could not tell him more and knew not much more myself.

CHAPTER 7

The Return of Sherlock Holmes

The following day dawned bright, and despite the tone of Culthorpe previously I presented myself at the breakfast table along with Brothers Orchard, Pisces, Shepherd, Culthorpe himself, Brother Chef and the new Brother Hive. I did not feel particularly welcome as far as Culthorpe was concerned but at least I made the number up to the required seven.

'Brother Orchard, have you left your dog with the horses?'

'Aye Brother Prior, that I have.'

Culthorpe made sure that even in the daylight there would be some warning of intruders before turning his ironic gaze upon me. 'Well, Brother Healer, I am a little surprised that you still grace our table but as you are with us I may as well explain to the brethren just who you really are. Brothers, meet Dr John Watson who has been known to you as Brother Healer. Of course being a qualified doctor I cannot say that he has been an impostor, but the same cannot be said of his friend, known to us as Brother

Hive: in fact, Sherlock Holmes who claims to be a detective. However, during the past week or so he has been not only unable to discover the identity of our adversary but even to prevent his deprivations.'

There was a buzz of startled converse and outbursts.

'Sherlock Holmes?'

'But he was too nervous to stay here!'

'Dr Watson, who is his Boswell?'

'Where is Holmes now?'

'Skulking in Baker Street, I'll be bound.'

'Fellow is an impostor!'

At these last words, spoken by Brother Chef, I all but exploded, venting upon that unfortunate friar words which I should really have reserved for Culthorpe who had fuelled Chef's unseemly comment.

I said, 'Brother Chef, I would remind you that you speak of the man who has solved a hundred and one seemingly unanswerable enigmas in the world of crime; the man who has rescued whole nations as well as celebrated personalities from seeming disaster. You speak of the world's first and still finest private investigator. Above all, you speak of my close and great friend!'

At that moment, as Brother Chef searched for a reply, there occurred one of those moments that can only be described as dramatic. Sherlock Holmes burst into the room, and standing there in his country tweeds, looking as unlike Brother Hive as can be imagined, said, 'Yes, and am I not fortunate to have such a friend as Dr Watson, for is a real friend not one who stands in your corner and defends you when all others have disowned you? Thank you, my dear Watson, for those words in my defence. However, now that Prior Culthorpe has seen fit to blow away the disguise which I wore in his service I have nothing to lose by speaking in my own right.'

There was silence, even Culthorpe sinking into his chair and shrugging his shoulders. Holmes was at his most magnetic and enigmatic as he continued.

'Brethren, let me give you a résumé of that which has happened in so far as Watson and I have been involved. To begin with your Prior, Septimus Culthorpe, called upon us at Baker Street with the news that two members of his order, the Secret Seven, had died under rather suspicious circumstances. It was decided that Watson and I would replace them in order both to restore your numbers to the required and mysterious seven, and also that we might investigate under the aliases of Hive and Healer with Watson seeing to your medical needs whilst I attempted to tend your bee hives. (Incidentally I fared quite well with the bees, for one without apiarists' experience.) I discovered that the two late and lamented brothers had died from the effects of cyanide, administered to them by way of a doctored adhesive upon the stamps with which they had been supplied in order that they answer letters, assured that they in turn would hear that which was to their advantage.'

Holmes paused and I offered him some coffee which he drank gratefully, giving the impression that his oration might be a long one. He resumed speaking.

'You see, Brothers, I am cutting all corners and leaving out a wealth of detail which can be later explained. Enough for now to say that we deduced that your tormentor had decided to take a slightly less drastic course in gaining his goal.'

Brother Shepherd dared to interrupt. 'Mr Holmes, what *was* his goal?'

'To rid Grimstone Priory of all its residents, by whatever means he could. He embarked upon a more general scare campaign as soon as he realized that any brothers eliminated individually might be replaced by others. So we had the horror of the slaughter of the lambs, the atrocity of the decapitated poultry and the phenomena, intended to be assumed supernatural but actually staged, of the ghostly riders from a previous century. Most recently we have had the wicked and wasteful destruction of the carp, only the largest and finest of them, from the pond. These had been captured by trawling in a mesh wide enough to allow the smaller ones to escape. Those of you who witnessed the result in the form of the butchered fish will have noted that although the destruction seemed senseless it had yet been performed by a skilled hand, as by an expert angler, chef or fishmonger.'

I noticed that Brother Chef looked particularly uncomfortable whilst the other friars sat wooden with amazement. Holmes continued.

'Despite the fact that the slaughter of the lambs and hens appeared to be less expert I have no reason to suppose any of these atrocities were performed by other than the same hand. A man can be expert in felling an ox yet inept at killing a pig.'

Culthorpe had been long silent but now he spoke up, seemingly not as repentant as one might expect him to be.

'Holmes you have explained quite a lot, and I am a little wiser than before, but only a little. There are two questions that I want you to answer me. Who is guilty, and why, above all *why* has he done these things? This vendetta against the Secret Seven appears pointless, unless there is one amongst us who has so enraged an enemy that he would destroy us all to eliminate his prey.'

Holmes replied, 'There is one among your brethren who was here during the time of his lordship, during the time when the famous family jewels disappeared.'

Culthorpe said, 'If that is so, and I much doubt it, what advantage is he after? If you know of the legendary jewels you will know of the circumstances of their disappearance from the tower. Assuming, and I take it that you do assume, that the jewels are still here, and that this person knows where they are, why does he not simply take them and leave? We have few rules, it would be easy enough for him, surely?'

Holmes continued, 'Let me explain that which I had intended to leave until later. This person was in the tower on the night that they disappeared. He was able to leave the tower unsuspected, for if he had the jewels he would have been carrying a bulky bag or even a small sack. Instead he was able to stand around with the rest as a search was made of the tower. He had hidden them in an extremely ingenious and well-planned manner.'

It was Brother Chef who asked, 'Do you mean that the jewels were hidden in the fabric of the tower's interior and might still be there?'

'No. The thief, however, did dispose of them in a manner

which would have enabled him to return and retrieve them.'

Culthorpe said, 'If he could not remove them on his person and there were no artefacts in the tower, and there were not, what do you suggest that he did, throw them out of the window?'

His enquiry was intended to be ironic but the enquirer was amazed at the answer which he got from Holmes. 'Exactly right, my dear Culthorpe, he threw them out of the window.'

There was a shocked silence, then Brother Orchard made a logical comment. 'The window is merely a slit, two or three inches wide.'

Holmes replied, 'He threw them out a few at a time.'

There was no irony in Culthorpe's next question. 'Into the moat?'

Holmes nodded to affirm. 'Yes, into the moat.'

Culthorpe thought for a moment then came back in a quite excited tone.

'But Holmes, the moat was drained shortly thereafter and no jewels were found. Even the mud was dredged, nothing had been in the moat which could have concealed them.'

'Except the carp!'

'The carp? They were transferred to the pond. They would scarcely have swallowed the jewels!'

'So one would think, but that is exactly what happened.'

Culthorpe had expressed his belief in Holmes's incompetence, but now he obviously began to doubt his sanity also.

'But good lord, man, fish do not eat rubies, diamonds and pearls. Brother Pisces will tell you that.'

Brother Pisces agreed. 'The Prior is right. Carp, the only breed of fish in the moat save for minnows, would eat those tiny fish and also insects and water weed. They will eat almost anything but certainly not jewels!'

Holmes said, 'Not intentionally, but disguised as food they well might have: did in fact. What, pray Brother Pisces, do you use to fish for carp: I mean what goes onto your hook?'

'Bread paste as a rule.'

'By bread paste you mean a sort of dough made from bread paste?'

'Exactly.'

Holmes paused; tired of standing he demanded a chair in which he sat, charging and lighting his pipe. Then he resumed.

'The man who made the famous jewels disappear went into the tower taking bread paste with him. He formed this around large individual jewels or two or three small ones. He formed and dropped these through the window slot so that they dropped into the moat to be eagerly snapped up by the carp. He could then walk out of that tower empty handed; the jewels evidently having disappeared from the face of the earth.'

I said, in support of Holmes's theory, 'The bread paste would be digested and pass through the fish; the jewels I imagine would stay in the crop.'

Holmes nodded. 'That was the theory, and the plan was one which involved the perpetrator returning to remove the fish from the moat at his leisure. However, he was detained, and when he was able to return to the area he found that the moat had been filled in. Then to his joy he discovered that the fish had been transferred to the pond. He knew that the very large fish would be those that had taken his expensive bait; the smaller fish would be their progeny so it would be easy to know which were those with the jewels in their crops.'

Culthorpe, astounded, eventually said, 'This man must have known a good deal about fish . . .'

Holmes snapped, 'Of course he did, and would have to have done in order to inaugurate the whole plan. But then many men do, through their trade or pastimes. For instance, Brother Chef knows a great deal about fish, especially carp. Is that not so, Brother Chef?'

Brother Chef started, then reddened as he said, 'I could scarcely be a chef without some knowledge of the anatomy of those cadavers which I need to dismember. Brother Healer will tell you that he also found his medical knowledge of use when sewing up a stuffed fish.'

I said, 'That is so, Holmes, and Brother Chef and I discovered what appeared to be a pearl in one carp; but he pointed out to me that only shellfish bear pearls and that it was perhaps ossified fish row. I sent it to you, Holmes, in a recent letter.'

'I received it, Watson, yet neglected to mention it in my reply. I should tell you that it was very useful in strengthening the theory already expounded which I had formed.'

Brother Shepherd timorously enquired, 'Might one ask what was the point of the destruction of my lambs, which had certainly not been dining upon jewels?'

Holmes answered, 'A good question: the lambs were

slaughtered not only as part of the general campaign of terror designed to empty the Priory, but to make the eventual slaughter of the carp seem equally pointless, an act of bestial vandalism.'

Brother Orchard enquired, 'You say that our adversary trawled the carp, yet he evidently only caught those large ones that had the jewels inside their crops.'

'Watson will affirm that the net we found was wide enough that all but the largest fish, survivors of the moat, might escape.'

Holmes sat back and a general unease set in. Culthorpe was the first to break this uneasy silence.

'But Holmes, you know what was done and why it was done, but you have no real idea, have you, as to who did it. Also you have allowed the jewels which evidently were practically presented to you on a plate to slip through your fingers!'

My friend worked hard upon his pipe for a full half-minute before he resumed his oration.

'Culthorpe, you are mistaken. You misjudge me and do me disservice with your words. I do know who the criminal is, and I have not let the Grimstone Priory jewels slip through my fingers.'

I could see that Culthorpe did not believe Holmes's words. He had got it into his mind that my friend's services had been of no help to him and the titbits that Holmes had thrown him had not quietened his appetite for the kind of results that he had evidently expected when he had appeared upon our doorstep at Baker Street. That first meeting seemed an age ago, so much having happened since. Murder by poison, the destruction of innocent creatures and the appearance of ghostly antagonists. All this aside from the sudden introduction to and involvement with the jewels in the tower; a formidable task for Sherlock Holmes but one which I knew he was equal to. I may have had some puzzlement at Holmes's handling of the case at one point, yet never had I doubted his ability to pull the whole thing together. Nor did I doubt his latest claims, however mysterious they sounded.

Culthorpe gazed steadily at Sherlock Holmes and asked, 'Mr Holmes, where then are the jewels at this exact moment?'

Casually, Holmes said, 'Why, they have been returned to the place where they should have been the whole time. They are in the tower!'

Culthorpe said nothing, but slowly he rose from his seat and started for the door. He stopped in front of the door itself, turned and said, 'I feel sure that you are making mockery, Holmes, but I will go along with your charade.'

He left the room and was away for several minutes. During that time questions were hurled at my friend by the brothers.

'How did you begin to suspect that the fish were a target?'

'It was a process of deduction and elimination. The use of the bread paste occurred to me when watching Brother Pisces angling for carp. The way the paste hid its grisly secret barb from the fish suggested that other things could be hidden in it. The rest was obvious, especially when my theory was compounded by Watson's discovery of the pearl.'

'You say there is one among us who was here in his lordship's day and returned, worked his way into our brotherhood just to bring about the recovery of the jewels? Why did he just not make some sort of a midnight raid upon the pond?'

'With seven friars in residence this would have been impossible to bring about unobserved. Some noise would have been caused. The foul deed was performed when all attention was directed toward the welfare of the horses, a decoy threat against them had been made. I followed up a number of enquiries in the village concerning his lordship's time. You would be surprised how informative the people at the library and the post office can be . . .'

He was interrupted by the entrance (or re-entrance) of Septimus Culthorpe. He was agitated or excited, or perhaps one could say both. Certainly his usual casual style of ironic communication had gone. He held a small sack which he raised aloft as he spoke.

'Mr Holmes, you were right; the Grimstone Priory jewels were back in the tower just as you said they would be. But how on earth did you know?'

Holmes chuckled. 'I could scarcely be ignorant of their presence when it was I who had put them there.'

Culthorpe looked as if he had been doused with a bucket of icy water.

'When did you place them there?'

'A few minutes before I entered this room.'

'When did you find them, and where?'

Holmes walked to the fireplace and quite deliberately knocked his pipe upon the inside of it. Then he refilled the pipe but to my relief did not attempt to go through the ritual of lighting it.

He said, 'I knew where they would be, in the cell of the brother who had taken them from the fish. I took them from there and placed them in the tower.'

It was I myself who asked the question which all save one wished to hear.

'Which of the brothers is the guilty person?'

Holmes smiled indulgently at me.

'Come, Watson, we can eliminate ourselves, the Prior Culthorpe, and . . .'

He was interrupted by Brother Orchard who asked, 'Whilst you are eliminating suspects, Mr Holmes, might I suggest that, with the greatest of respect *all* present should be considered, other than yourself and Dr Watson? I know that it was our Prior who called upon you to investigate, but there has always been complete equality within the Secret Seven.'

Holmes considered. 'Very well then, but this is academic for I know the identity of the culprit. He made a mistake when he obtained a net of suitable gauge for his purpose and decided to hide it in the apiary shed, thinking to take advantage of my absence and knowing enough of bees himself to have no belief in my fable of the latent swarm within. He also knew that the new Brother Hive was seldom in the vicinity, being even less of an apiarist than am I myself.'

Brother Shepherd intervened. 'Mr Holmes, how could you know of this when you were yourself absent from the priory for the past week, communicating with Dr Watson by means of the penny post.'

Holmes shook his head. 'My absence was a ruse. I returned and took up residence in the shed, sleeping therein by night and keeping myself out of sight during the day.'

Brother Orchard asked, 'How did you manage that?'

'Some of the time I was in the copse, but much of the time I sat quietly wearing the protective clothing and mask, knowing that from a distance it would appear to be simply propped up as it had been for some time. In that way I was able to observe quite a lot.'

Brother Pisces asked, 'How did you survive?'

'Easily, for I had the aid of my young friend Billy, who is the pageboy at 221B Baker Street. He obtained lodgings in the village and discreetly saw to my needs by bringing food and clean linen. When I had observed the brother busied with the net I also remembered the pearl that Watson sent to me in a letter which was forwarded from Baker Street. He told me how it had been extracted from the carp when Brother Chef had instructed him in the expert opening of that fish with the knife.'

I started. I realized that I should have associated Brother Chef's expert wielding of a fish-gutting knife with the happening at the pond. I was about to speak when Holmes made my intended utterance redundant.

'However, it was not Brother Chef whom I observed with the net.'

Brother Shepherd fairly exploded. 'Mr Holmes, I myself visited the vicinity of the hives during the period in question. I was seeking the new Brother Hive but he was not there. Curiosity made me approach the shed and peer into its window.'

Holmes reassured him. 'I observed your coming and going, Brother Shepherd, for I was encased in the apiarist's armour at the time.'

Brother Orchard said, 'You have narrowed things down to Brother Pisces and myself then, but I can see one other possibility; you have said little regarding your replacement. We have your word, I suppose, that he is above reproach, but as I know of my own innocence and feel sure concerning that of Brother Pisces I can see no other direction to cast my suspicion.'

Holmes had assured us that he knew the identity of the culprit and yet I quite failed to see how either Brother Orchard or Brother Pisces could be guilty. The gentle Orchard was unthinkable as a criminal, and Brother Pisces had tended the carp with such dedication that I could not believe that he would have destroyed them. I spoke up for them both at this point, hoping that my intervention would help to speed up the nerve-wracking drama that Holmes appeared to savour. I said, 'I appreciate Brother Orchard's point, Holmes, even I know nothing about your deputy hive keeper.'

Holmes stood and surveyed the grounds through a window, his back turned to us. Why, oh why was he so determined to prevaricate.

But at length he spun around and said, 'There is no point in my giving you the new brother's pedigree when I can tell you that the guilty man is Brother Pisces!'

A general gasp followed this statement, but I was intrigued to notice that Brother Pisces remained extremely calm. Eventually he rose slowly to his feet and spoke.

'So, Mr Sherlock Holmes, great detective, you are accusing me of a series of crimes and acts of bestiality. Yet the good Prior and my fellow brethren know that what you say cannot be. You suggest that you saw me coming and going with a net but through that mesh mask you could have mistaken another for myself. Moreover, if you found jewels in my cell you forget that another could have placed them there.'

Holmes snapped, 'But I know that another did not; everything fits together.'

'Maybe in your eyes, but you would need to convince my brothers of the Secret Seven to make your accusations stand up in a court of law. That is, if it ever reaches that stage, for you have no right to detain me. You may be a detective, but you are not a policeman!'

At the moment these words had been spoken there occurred one of the most dramatic occurrences that I remember being witness to. The locum Brother Hive, he of the beard and luxuriant hair arose, removed from his head a wig and from his chin a false beard and revealed the homely features and thinning hair of Inspector Lestrade of Scotland Yard.

He spoke firmly and in a stern tone. 'Godfrey Carrington, known also as Brother Pisces, I arrest you on suspicion of murder and destruction of livestock. Anything you say will be taken down and used in evidence . . .'

Brother Pisces was obviously shocked by this turn of events yet was still calm enough to demand, 'Who, sir, might you be?'

'I am Inspector George Lestrade of Scotland Yard!'

'Oh, so you too have been spying upon me? Well, Inspector, you will have to catch me first!'

Having uttered these words he made for the entrance door with a surprising turn of speed, but his way was barred by a burly constable who laid hands upon him.

Holmes said to Brother Pisces, 'Carrington, I took the precaution of sending Billy for the village constable as soon as I knew that the jewels were in your cell as I suspected them to be. Then I placed them in the tower and the rest you know. Gentlemen and brethren, I must now apologize for the very long drawn-out recitation of that which could have so easily been said in one sentence, but you see I had to play for time in order to ensure Carrington's arrest. Once I had observed the arrival of Billy with the constable I was able of course to hasten my address and reach my finale. I leave it all in your hands now, Lestrade. Oh and by the way, Culthorpe, I am afraid the jewels will be required as evidence.'

Culthorpe merely nodded in a dazed fashion and, once Lestrade had changed from his friar's habit to his city attire, he and the constable left for the village police station in Culthorpe's dogcart. They were driven by Brother Shepherd, and when he returned in the vehicle without his passengers he joined the rest of us in the nearest to a celebration that one could expect under such circumstances.

Brother Chef managed to produce a few delicacies and there were flagons of beer and cider. But before the celebrating had really begun Culthorpe drew us both aside and began to make what was to be a whole series of apologies.

He obviously hardly knew where to begin.

'My dear Mr Holmes, what can I say except that I am so sorry to have doubted your abilities. But you can imagine how I felt when atrocities and bizarre incidents seemed to occur without any sign of your being able to prevent them. But of course I was ignorant of so much that you were doing. I had no idea that your deputy was Inspector Lestrade!'

'I could not tell you lest by word or deed you should unwittingly betray his presence. If it is any comfort to you, Watson was as amazed as anyone when he removed his disguise.'

I nodded, and said, 'Moreover, I was quite unaware of Holmes's return to the area, thinking him still in Baker Street.'

Culthorpe was surprised at this. 'Heavens, Holmes, you keep your findings from members of your own team as much as from those that you stalk. My delight with the outcome will be reflected in the fee that I pay you.'

Holmes shook his head and waved an admonishing hand.

'My charges never vary save where I omit them entirely, as I believe I mentioned to you once before?'

'Yes you did, but it seems like an age ago now.'

My friend looked thoughtful. 'Speaking of monetary gain, my dear Culthorpe, the ownership of the jewels may be clouded in doubt. I believe I learned during my investigations that the old lord died intestate, in which case you might well have gained more of a bargain even than you thought you had when you obtained this property at such a reasonable price.'

Culthorpe, still rather hangdog in his manner towards

Holmes, said, 'Any good fortune that I gain in that direction will be ploughed into the improvement of this house and farm for the benefit and well-being of the brothers of the Secret Seven.'

I could not help but to say, 'It is my sincere hope then, my dear Culthorpe, that the seven can remain secret. Journalists being what they are I somewhat doubt it.'

Holmes scolded me. 'Oh come, Watson, let us not spoil the party by putting the cart before the horse. Shall we join in the festivities?'

We returned to where the others were enjoying a brief respite from their somewhat Spartan day-to-day existence. I looked around them and thought what splendid fellows they were. But then I had thought that Brother Pisces was a splendid fellow too!

'Here, Doctor, come and have a slice of pork pie!'

It was Billy who spoke, his cheery face flushed with the unaccustomed pint of cider that he had consumed.

Holmes shook a finger at him and said, 'You wait until Mrs Hudson hears about all this, young man!'

Billy's face suddenly returned to its pale city dweller's pallor. 'You wouldn't tell on me would you, guv'nor?'

We both assured him that we would not.

It was quite a jolly gathering, the friars with their instruments eventually striking up a jolly tune or two, or three.

'Brethren, in our revels we have forgotten to consider a rather important matter . . .'

Culthorpe had been diplomatic enough to choose a lull in the jollifications to address them. Once he had their attention he said, 'You will realize, I am sure, that despite the lifting of the burden of living in fear, we still have a problem. We are back to a reduction in our numbers once more and require three good men and true to bring our numbers back to the required and mysterious seven.'

Billy looked at me and grinned, seemingly about to raise a hand to volunteer. I admonished him at once.

'Billy . . . certainly not!'

CHAPTER 8

Once More the Secret Seven

I had been right in my prediction that the journalists would have a field day when Carrington was charged with murder and other serious crimes. Even the sedate *Thunderer* could not help but be intrigued enough with the case that involved seven hooded friars who were part of a secret society. But then many were the headlines in the less sedate broad sheets . . .

THE PERIL OF THE SEVEN HOODED MEN
THE SECRET SOCIETY NO LONGER DOOMED
SECRET SOCIETY SEEKS REPLACEMENTS

Also I fear there were stories and headlines which featured my friend:

SHERLOCK HOLMES AND THE SECRET SEVEN
FAMOUS DETECTIVE SAVES SECRET SOCIETY

And even,

SHERLOCK SAVES SECRET SEVEN SOCIETY

Of course both Holmes and I were required to give evidence at the Old Bailey where the famous hanging judge Burroughs presided. It was a case which had a conclusion that was foregone. But strange to relate there were those who spoke up for Carrington; a great uncle, a maiden aunt and believe it or not dear reader, Brothers Orchard and Shepherd. Neither of these kind souls could deny the wickedness of his acts, or the fact that they had performed them, but both made sure that his seeming acts of industry and friendship were recorded as well.

The judge, Burroughs, in his summing-up for the jury said, 'If you have listened to all of the evidence as carefully as I, then I quite fail to see how you can return other than a verdict of guilty.'

Strangely the jury were out for quite a considerable time and one can only surmise that they questioned the sanity of Carrington despite a medical report which had claimed him to be and to have been at the time that he had performed his dreadful crimes, quite, quite sane. I admit that I found this difficult to believe myself. However, eventually the jury assembled once more and returned a verdict of guilty.

Judge Burroughs demanded, 'And that is the verdict of you all?'

'It is, m'lud!'

I had read so many times of the drama created when a judge donned the black cap but I had never actually witnessed it before and I admit that my blood ran cold despite my knowledge of his criminality.

Judge Burroughs said, 'Godfrey Carrington, you have been tried by a jury of your peers upon two cases of cold-blooded murder, and on numerous other charges of acts of evil and bestiality. However I will sentence you only upon the charges of murder. The sentence is that you will be taken from here to a place of imprisonment and from thence to another place where after a designated number of days you will be hung by the neck until you are dead. May God have mercy upon your soul!'

Betwixt being found guilty and this sentence of death, Carrington had been asked if there was anything that he wished to say. He had answered in the affirmative and said, 'Had I continued with my original plan and had the patience to carry it through to the end I would not be standing here now; but I lost patience and tried to bring about a conclusion too quickly, thanks to the interference of Holmes, the meddling busybody!'

There was no sorrow, no apologies, and no cries for heavenly forgiveness. He was quite unrepentant.

During the three weeks or so that went before his execution we were involved with another matter for Culthorpe: that of his right to the Grimstone Priory jewels. But it was a mere formality or rather it would have been without the notoriety of the murder trial. But even this could not long hold up a court finding for Culthorpe.

To give him his due, and despite Holmes's words upon the subject, he did once more give my friend the chance of accepting a very large financial reward in addition to the fee that he had paid. But Holmes would accept nothing for himself but dared to suggest that a trust fund should be set up for the Irregulars, to be called upon as and when any of them should be in dire need.

Godfrey Carrington was not the sort of man that one should have lost much sleep over, yet as the day of the execution drew nearer one could not help but experience a queasy feeling in the pit of the stomach.

During that period, three weeks of trying to live a normal life whilst yet knowing that one had been responsible in part for the sentence, was that stuff that nightmares are made of. Sherlock Holmes appeared to be entirely unaffected by the thought of that sinister day that must inevitably dawn. He had experienced it all before, as indeed had I, though this made it no easier for me. On the eve of Carrington's execution I paced the sitting-room at Baker Street whilst Holmes tried to read his newspaper.

'Watson, can you not relax and resume your usual activities? If not, I wish you would take yourself off and perhaps pace in the park or in Oxford Street. We both know what will occur at first light in the morning and that no miscarriage of justice is involved. Carrington thoroughly deserves to be hung!'

'Yes, Holmes, I appreciate that and will as you suggest remove myself to the great outdoors that my fidgeting shall not trouble you further. But these occasions do bring home to one that a man hung and his execution read about in the newspaper is no mere statistic. They will you know actually take a man from his cell, march him to a scaffold, blindfold him, place a noose about his neck and then spring the trap. He will then hang by the neck until dead: but how long will that take and how do we know what will pass through his mind?'

'Let us hope, Watson, that there will be some feelings of

remorse and pity for the sufferings, however short, of his two victims. I will not count the lambs, hens and fish; for the butcher and the fishmonger lose little sleep.'

I was still uncomfortable with this whole business of a life for a life. Certainly at least we knew that there had been no miscarriage of justice involved regarding Carrington, yet the principle did not, or does not, go easily in my mind. The brisk walk in Regent's Park, however, did its job in making my mind turn to other matters, albeit those still connected to the Secret Seven. I lived again that dramatic moment when Inspector Lestrade had appeared as if by magic where there had been Brother Hive. Yet another detail which Holmes had kept a close secret, even from myself. I had meant to speak with Lestrade afterwards, for I marvelled at his spending so much of his time at Holmes's request, yet supposed that his reputation at Scotland Yard would hardly have suffered through the result.

It so happened that on my way back to Baker Street I passed a group of people with placards which they carried upon staves of wood which proclaimed: SAVE CARRINGTON and ABOLISH HANGING. I wondered who these people were that they had the time and inclination to parade their beliefs through the streets in this manner? They looked at a glance to be just ordinary people, yet if one examined them closely one could see that they were a little different from the passing herd. There were matron ladies, severely dressed, of the sort who might be otherwise engaged in charitable work. There were clerics, as I would have expected, but there also appeared the downtrodden, the shabby, the fanatic even whose wild eyes and wild gestures betrayed them. I mentioned this parade to Holmes upon my return and he nodded with understanding.

'Many times I have encountered these groups, Watson, and upon the morrow outside the prison they will be thick upon the ground. I respect their views of course but I would wager that any one of them might suffer a change of conscience should a murderer slay their nearest and dearest. Might they not consult Sherlock Holmes to bring the sinner to justice and would they then bemoan his passing at the hands of Jack Ketch?'

It was of course the old question which is put to those who refuse to take up arms in time of war in defence of their country when we say to them 'If a lunatic attacked your wife with a sledgehammer would you not hasten to her aid, despite your pacifist beliefs?' But the argument is such that it cannot be won.

Public executions had of course been long abolished at the time of which I write, yet crowds would still gather outside the prison upon the morrow and I found myself strangely lured into being one of them; and so it was that before dawn I made my way to the prison gates. I had never been a part of such a gathering before and it was an experience that I will never forget nor intend to repeat. There were many people of the kind that I had seen in Regent's Park, but in addition there were many others: the curious, the sadistic, and even those who intended to profit through the event. These were peddlers, not just of the usual buns, pork pies and sweetmeats, but those who sold bizarre souvenirs of the hanging; gruesome models of a gallows and portraits of Carrington which varied enormously in their accuracy. There was also a small, sinister-looking man sporting a battered top hat who was offering small wooden figures in friars' robes. He chanted, 'Take home a model of the Mad M

onk to remember the day! The Mad Monk . . . lifelike and natural!'

The whole scene reminded me of Charles Dickens's perfect descriptions of such macabre events. We believe that we are civilized in this day and age when we are approaching a brave new century; yet below our civilized gloss is still a blood lust which many find it hard to disguise.

'My dear Dr Watson, I wondered if you might be here.'

It was Culthorpe, in his prior's robes and a look of piety upon his face. Had he come to weep crocodile tears over the execution for which he was in some measure responsible.

He added, 'Sherlock Holmes did not wish to join you, then, in seeing his task finally completed?'

I said, 'No, but Holmes is an enigmatic character; he seldom shares his feelings with others, even with myself, his closest friend.'

As the bell tolled and began to strike the hour a hush fell over the crowd and Culthorpe dropped his head as if in prayer. Then as the final bell had chimed he looked up and said, 'I was not praying for Carrington, Watson.'

I was surprised. 'Were you not?'

He said, 'No, rather I was praying for Brother Pisces!'